Her heart sped up.

She ordered it to stop that nonsense, right now.

Her heart had other ideas. When Grant climbed out of the car and crossed the drive, the sight of him, rugged and strong, dressed in working man's clothes, tugged at her.

"You're shoveling?"

"Just finished."

"I'd have done this for you." He reached out and tucked her hair back behind her ear, then indicated the walks with his gaze, but didn't move his hand. "It would be my pleasure, Em."

The strength of his callused hand against her cheek, against her ear, sent warmth through her. "Grant, I—"

"You're beautiful with snowflakes in your hair." He spoke softly, tenderly. "But you're beautiful without the snowflakes, too."

"Grant…"

"Em." He whispered her name then gathered her into a long, warm embrace, the kind of hug a woman would cherish for all her days.

"I'll see you in the morning, okay?" She stepped back, because if she didn't, she might linger in the yard forever, lost in the moment.

Multipublished, bestselling author **Ruth Logan Herne** loves God, her country, her family, dogs, chocolate and coffee! Married to a very patient man, she lives in an old farmhouse in upstate New York and thinks possums should leave the cat food alone and snakes should always live outside. There are no exceptions to either rule! Visit Ruthy at ruthloganherne.com.

Books by Ruth Logan Herne

Love Inspired

Grace Haven

An Unexpected Groom
Her Unexpected Family

Kirkwood Lake

The Lawman's Second Chance
Falling for the Lawman
The Lawman's Holiday Wish
Loving the Lawman
Her Holiday Family
Healing the Lawman's Heart

Men of Allegany County

Small-Town Hearts
Mended Hearts
Yuletide Hearts
A Family to Cherish
His Mistletoe Family

Big Sky Centennial

His Montana Sweetheart

Visit the Author Profile page at Harlequin.com for more titles.

Her Unexpected Family

Ruth Logan Herne

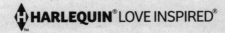

LOVE INSPIRED BOOKS

Recycling programs
for this product may
not exist in your area.

ISBN-13: 978-0-373-81926-3

Her Unexpected Family

www.Harlequin.com

Printed in U.S.A.

Her Unexpected Family

Ruth Logan Herne

HARLEQUIN® LOVE INSPIRED®

Recycling programs
for this product may
not exist in your area.

LOVE INSPIRED BOOKS

ISBN-13: 978-0-373-81926-3

Her Unexpected Family

To my beautiful daughter Beth:
You are a blessing and a delight to us.
Thank you for being a constant source of
love, light and encouragement.
And the four grandkids are a total bonus!

Acknowledgments

A special thanks to Jean Cosgriff, Ed Hall,
Donna Kocienski and Kathy Pittaway for their
love and help during my years at Bridal Hall.
Your warmth and humor made it an
absolute pleasure to work there!
And to the constant efforts of the Town of Parma
Highway Department, always working to keep
roads safe and clear. Your example helped me
shape this delightful story. Every time you get
behind the wheel of one of those big plows or
machines, you're a hero to so many of us.
Thank you!

Let all bitterness and wrath and anger and clamor and slander be put away from you, along with all malice. Be kind to one another, tenderhearted, forgiving one another, as God in Christ forgave you.
—Ephesians 4:31–32

Chapter One

I can't break this appointment again, Grant McCarthy thought as he bundled the twins into their car seats. He'd already put the wedding planner off twice.

Timmy gazed up at him, round-eyed, then smacked him upside the head with a plastic truck. For a little guy, the two-year-old packed a mean punch.

Dolly squalled from the moment he started carrying her toward the car, as if being strapped in made her want to lash out irrationally. Being two and developmentally delayed, instant meltdowns had become a chronic reaction. While Tim looked on, Dolly blubbered nonstop, and pools of water seemed to come from everywhere.

"Dowwy's sad." Timmy gazed across the backseat of the minivan. His lower lip quivered in sympathy. His eyes started to fill, and Grant knew he had to act fast.

"She's fine, Timmers, I promise," Grant reassured his little son. He trotted around the front of the car, climbed in and started the engine. "She hates being tied down, that's all."

He smiled at Tim through the rearview mirror, but didn't dare glance Dolly's way. She'd stopped crying for the moment, but if he made eye contact, she'd start all over again. It was bad enough that his aunt came down with the same virus the twins had shared a few weeks ago, but to get it today, when he was supposed to meet with the wedding planner for his sister Christa's wedding, spelled disaster. On top of that, Aunt Tillie had chewed him out for attempting to plan the wedding, take care of two babies and a house while running the town highway department. She told him he was downright foolish to even try.

At the moment, he was inclined to agree.

He drove into the shopping district of Grace Haven, New York, a quaint town tucked in the picturesque Finger Lakes region. He made a right turn into The Square. Originally a small-town hub surrounding a cozy central park, The Square was now a shopping destination beloved by tourists and locals. The predicted rain hadn't hit yet, and he hoped for a roadside parking space along the popular series of shops.

Unfortunately, not a single spot was free, and that meant he'd have to maneuver both kids through the back parking lot once he got them unlatched and he was already ten minutes late.

He hated when people held him up on his job. Time was money and expectations in local government were high, just as they should be. But here he was, doing the exact same thing to whatever Gallagher sister they assigned him. As he hopped out of the SUV, he hoped it wouldn't be the beauty queen. After his upscale wife had left him and two babies high and dry, he'd had enough of appearance-loving women to last a lifetime.

He snugged Dolly into his shoulder and ushered Timmy through the lot as fast as stubby toddler legs would go. The west wind bit sharp, a sure sign of the coming winter. Once wind and cold and snow hit full force, his road crews would work nonstop to keep the valley and upland roads safe for travel, a busy and sometimes frantic season for northern highway departments. And a wedding, on top of it—

But he was honored to help his sister. He loved her courage and tenacity. He loved her.

Timmy caught his foot on the edge of an all-weather mat as they stepped through the door.

He sprawled onto the floor and burst into tears partially because he was brush burned, but mostly because it was nap time. The timing had seemed ideal when Kate & Company had suggested a weekend meeting. A Saturday afternoon, two kids napping, his aunt to babysit them and he'd take care of getting things going for his sister's special day.

Wanna hear God laugh? Tell Him your plans. His mother's old adage hung true, especially today.

He bent low. Allison Kellor noticed him from the gracious, formal entry facing the street. She offered a sympathetic wince as he stood, gathering Timmy into his free arm. He strode forward, carrying both toddlers, and crossed the elegant entry as if he belonged there.

"Grant McCarthy?"

He turned toward the voice and took a deep breath. The beauty queen, of course, looking absolutely, perfectly put together from the thick auburn waves of hair to the designer outfit and red high heels.

Doomed.

He didn't belong there. She did. And maybe Aunt Tillie was right—maybe he was stupid to think he could handle spinning multiple plates in the air. A wave of negativity rose inside him.

He forced it down and faced the beautiful

woman descending the curved, open stairway and said, "We made it."

"So I see."

For a split second he was tempted to make a run for it. But then the redhead came closer. She held out her arms. Normally effusive Timmy ducked his head, probably struck dumb by her beauty.

Her good looks weren't lost on Grant. This woman was downright appealing and absolutely lovely. That gave him reason enough to maintain his distance. He'd spent years thinking appearances mattered, then one broken heart later, he learned they shouldn't really matter at all.

"Ba." Dolly peeked up at the woman and did something she hadn't done in a long time. She opened her arms to someone other than him, Aunt Tillie and the occupational therapist that stopped by the day care facility twice a week. "Oh, ba."

"Come here, precious." The redhead didn't seem to care that Dolly's face was blotched from anger, tears and ghastly unmentionable things she'd smeared on Grant's coat. Her little jacket was dotted with something unidentifiable and had remnants of vanilla wafer crushed into the zipper, but when the former beauty queen took her, Dolly wove two tiny hands into the prettiest red hair he'd ever seen and chortled. "Ba! Ba!"

"Red." The woman ducked her head while Dolly explored her hair, then peeked up at the girl and pulled a strand of that long, gorgeous hair sideways for the little one to see. "Red hair."

"Wad!" Dolly laughed, amused, as if the wedding planner got her joke.

"Miss Gallagher, I'm sorry we're late." He made a face of regret and nodded toward the clock. "We missed the first appointment because Dolly had that nasty upper respiratory virus that's been going around. Then Timmy got it. And now, my Aunt Tillie—"

"Tillie Gibson, right?" she asked, and nodded toward Allison. "My mom and Allison handled her daughter's wedding last spring. I heard it was wonderful."

"They were thrilled with how it all came out," he admitted. "And that's what made me think of Kate & Company for my sister Christa's wedding. She and her fiancé, Spencer, are both deployed, they're pursuing air force careers, and I wanted to make this wedding nice for her. I know these aren't exactly ideal conditions."

The redhead frowned. "Not ideal conditions? Why?"

She acted as if she really didn't have a clue and that made Grant drag a hand through his hair. It seemed thinner on top right now, and why would he notice that at this moment? Was it because of the drop-dead beauty standing there, holding his precious child and looking up at him with the most amazing bright brown eyes he'd ever seen?

Yes, which was ridiculous because he'd been out of the dating game for years and it wasn't a game he ever intended to play again. "Well, the kids. With Tillie sick…"

"We'll talk around them."

She had to be kidding. He looked beyond her to the classy office that smacked of good taste, not sticky fingers. "Do you—"

"I'm Emily." She kept Dolly snugged in her arm, looking quite comfortable with the child as she extended her right hand. "The middle one."

Oh, he knew who she was all right. He might be ten years older than she was, but the whole town had watched and cheered as Emily Gallagher brought home first prize in pageant after pageant as a teen, then as a woman.

He glanced around, doubtful. "You really think this will be okay?"

"Pull up a spot on the carpet." He wasn't sure how someone could manage to sink to the floor gracefully while holding a messy toddler, but Emily Gallagher did it with finesse. Once down, she set Dolly on her bottom, then worked the cookie-crusted zipper from the jacket with nimble fingers. "Allison, can you do a quick sweep for anything reachable and breakable?"

"I'm on it. And here's a pen so you can do hard-copy notes. We'll transfer them later."

"Post-babies!" She laughed, and when she did, Grant's blood pressure dropped to a more normal level even though his heart sped up.

She wasn't patronizing him. She wasn't treating Dolly different from Tim, and for reasons he'd never be able to explain, Dolly had fallen in love with Emily at first sight, and Dolly didn't like too many people.

"So." She picked up the pen, flipped open the notebook and faced him as he and Timmy settled onto the floor nearby. "We talked about a February wedding on the phone. Is that still the plan?"

"January, now," he told her as he worked Timmy's jacket off. "The second Saturday." The minute he was free of his father's help, the little boy got up and raced around the spacious room.

"I'll keep an eye out from here," Allison promised from her area. "You guys see what you can accomplish."

"You told me on the phone that Christa and Spencer are regular, straightforward people. Neither one likes too much glitz and glamour."

"No, ma'am. They're simple, hardworking types. Most of my family's the same way."

He must have sounded brusque, because her left brow rose fractionally, but her voice stayed matter-of-fact. "While several of the local venues close for the winter, most stay open as needed, making a January venue fairly easy to secure."

"Of course the problem is, we run into storms, then." He frowned, because in his line of work, weather always took primary consideration. "There's no way around it, though. That's the only time they can arrange leave together."

"Have generators waiting…" she murmured as she made a note on the pad.

He stared at her. "You're serious?"

"Of course. It's sensible, right?"

"Yes, but—" He looked around the beautiful trappings of her mother's business and shrugged. "You surprised me, that's all."

She paused her pen, looked him in the eye and held his gaze. "Pretty doesn't mean nonfunctional."

Ouch.

She'd nailed his opinion in one quick lesson, and while he was sure she meant well, he'd run the gamut with his wife of nearly nine years. Serenity had lived for appearances. Not so much at first. She'd been a local news anchor for the Rochester area and had been crazy popular. He'd thought she was happy.

She wasn't.

As their economic status rose, so did her penchant for success.

They'd put off having children because the timing had never been quite right. Her job, his job, education, job security… And then suddenly they were pregnant with twins.

Grant had been ecstatic.

Serenity had looked trapped from the moment the stick changed color until the day she piled her suitcases and a picture of Timmy into her car and drove to a new job in Baltimore. He pushed the image aside.

"Backup generators would be great."

"Do we want a church for the ceremony?"

"Christa has always loved the abbey your uncle runs. I ran the new date by him and he said it was clear, so I was thinking a two o'clock wedding. Is that a good time?"

"Perfect, especially with the decreased daylight in winter." She made a quick note as Dolly tried to grab her pen. "Hey, you." She laughed into Dolly's sweet, round face and then up at him. "So that's Tim." She pointed to the little boy. "And this is?"

"Dolly."

"Perfect!" She laughed and made wide eyes at Dolly. Dolly shrieked in delight, clapped her hands together and giggled out loud. "She's like a little doll. Great name."

"It's really Dolores Marie for my mother," he said. "I thought Dolly would be a cute nickname for her. My mother died before she was born, so it's a nice way to carry on the family names."

"It's marvelous." Dolly stood up, looking steady, but when she went to chase after her brother, she stopped and went from happy-go-lucky toddler to instant anger. She stuck out her lower lip, stomped her foot twice and glared across the room at her twin. When Timmy ignored her, she stomped again, scowled at her father and burst into tears.

Grant stood and carried her across the room, then set her down next to Timmy. He came back, sat down and waited for Emily to proceed.

"What's she going to do when he moves?" Emily asked, and something in her voice tweaked Grant's protective juices.

"Crawl after him. Or get mad."

"Oh."

One word. One tiny, two-letter word, but it was like he'd just been tried and convicted in the court of Gallagher. "You have a better way?"

She looked from Dolly to him, then said, "Walking's always good."

"She can't," he explained and thought he'd gain sympathy because even though Dolly's chromosomal defects weren't blatantly obvious to others, they were real enough.

Emily Gallagher did a slow, thorough look of him, then his daughter, then back. "You mean she won't."

"She's afraid."

Emily's expression said she'd figured that out herself. "Won't stop being afraid until she does it, I expect."

Irritation mushroomed inside him, like it did every time someone expected Dolly to be normal. She wasn't normal, not by society's standards. He understood that, so what was wrong with the rest of the world? "You have kids, Miss Gallagher?"

She shook her head.

"But you know everything there is to know about kids, I suppose? Especially kids with Dolly's condition?" He was tired of fielding questions from people who doubted Dolly's diagnosis of Down syndrome, just because her face looked more normal than most affected children.

"Actually, I do," she answered easily as she flipped the page. "I spent summers here, helping my mother, but my off-campus job during the school year was working in a children's group home. I spent four years on staff there. We had several clients with limited abilities, some with

Down syndrome, and I was honored to work with the wide spectrum of effect. I might have majored in business and fashion design, but I worked with therapists, clinicians and the kids. It's scary for a normally functioning kid to take those first steps, too, but parents don't discourage them."

He hated that she made perfect sense, because Aunt Tillie had been telling him the same thing. Did he want Dolly to be stymied by her limitations? Or did he want her to reach for the stars?

He scowled, because this wasn't open for discussion. He wanted his perfectly imperfect daughter to be safe. End of story. "Let's get back to the wedding planning, shall we?"

"Of course." She answered smoothly, but that was to be expected of a woman who used to field pageant judge questions with grace and a welcoming smile. She smiled now, but something in her eyes said he'd just flunked a test he didn't even know he'd been taking.

Emily Gallagher was pretty sure she needed her life back, a life of fabrics and fashions made to flatter the everyday woman.

Schmoozing overprotective fathers hadn't made her short list, ever. And yet, here she was, helping out with the family business because she was needed. She was fine with that part.

It was the bridezilla factor she disliked, and in this case, the "brother-zilla."

He'd looked downright appealing striding down that hall, toting an adorable twin in each arm.

Tall, strong and vigorous with dark wavy hair and gray-blue eyes. Out of place and yet perfectly natural as he lugged two toddlers into the reception area of her mother's wedding and event-planning office. And yes...smokin' hot, even though he was older than her by a decade.

Emily knew his story. Most of the town knew Grant's story because he was a public figure. Head of the highway department and public works, he was the man in charge for blizzards, floods, road collapses and season-to-season road repair.

Privacy was nonexistent for town officials. She knew that firsthand, her father having been the town police chief for decades. Living center stage was one of the downsides of small-town life. The entire area knew Grant's wife had walked out on him after having twins, one of whom had Down syndrome. And here he was, trying to juggle raising two kids and planning his sister's wedding while she and her fiancé were deployed.

Sympathy welled within her, and she drew

on that initial reaction when the guy caved to Dolly's miniature temper tantrum.

Not her kid. Not her business.

Her sister Rory came through the back door just then. Mags, their mother's spunky Yorkshire terrier, raced in with her. Mags spotted the kids, spun around in circles, jumped up on her hind legs and yapped hello.

"Does she bite?" Grant asked.

Emily raised her eyes slowly as Rory scooped up the Yorkie. "Only on command."

He narrowed his gaze, holding hers, and she wondered if he was going to get up and walk out. He didn't, but she was pretty sure he was tempted to. "Keeping these two safe isn't an easy task, Miss Gallagher."

"Whereas my dad always told us life was meant to be lived, challenge by challenge."

He put up his hands as if conceding a battle. "Well, runway walking can be considered dangerous, especially in high heels."

She froze.

So did Rory and Allison, as if they couldn't believe what he just said. Even the dog paused, but then Emily burst out laughing. The thought that she still had to justify her Miss Rochester and Miss New York pageant wins years later was absolutely hilarious. Obviously, her years as a major department store buyer were inconsequential in her hometown. "Fortunately, wedding planning is rarely lethal, so we're all good. What kind of budget are we looking at for Captain McCarthy's wedding?"

He had the grace to look uncomfortable.

He reached out and steered Dolly away from the stairs. "My mother created a fund specifically for this wedding before she passed away." He named a figure that allowed her some latitude, and as Emily went through the list of typical questions, he relaxed somewhat. Of course Rory and Mags were now amusing the toddlers, and that was a big help as Allison put the finishing touches on a planning board for an upcoming reception at an esteemed vineyard.

Emily laid out a bunch of brochures before him. "Mr. McCarthy, your job makes you uniquely familiar with the area."

He nodded, but didn't ask her to call him by his first name like a normal person would. She wasn't sure why that irked her, but it did.

"Weather might go our way, or it might not. We've had some of our worst storms in January, ranging from blizzards to ice storms, to driving rain storms that caused road flooding," she said.

"I can't change the date."

She acknowledged that smoothly. "I realize that, but I want you to have a clear picture as you make choices. Choosing a hillside setting can be lovely if it's blanketed in snow, but horrific if we've got icy conditions and no one can get to the venue. Likewise, the lakeshore options are stunning, but a mild winter where the lake doesn't freeze can cause road flooding if we get a storm that weekend. If your department has to close roads, it means no one can access the reception."

"Gotcha." He studied the brochures, then angled a look to her, and when he did, she had to remind her heart that he was a somewhat presumptuous jerk who overprotected his children, no matter how gorgeous his smoke-toned eyes were. "A town reception venue would be a better choice, don't you think?"

She shrugged. "I hate to discourage you from the others, because they're gorgeous, but it's important for our clients to see the whole picture when they plan an event. On the other hand..." She slanted a smile his way, and for just a moment, he held that look, almost as if interested... which was completely preposterous, of course. "You *are* the head of the highway department, your people are skilled at keeping roads clear and the few mishaps that have occurred are rare. So now it's up to you. Shall we set up a time to go see some of these lakeside venues? I've got

Monday free. Is it possible for you to get some time off?"

"There's no availability to see them on a Saturday?"

She shook her head. "Fall and the holidays are crazy busy. They're booked solid. We could arrange for evening visits if time off is difficult. I can call the ones that interest you, arrange a food tasting and a tour."

"What evenings are you free next week?" he asked.

She should lie.

She should pretend to be crazy busy with a social life that overflowed into the following year, but the fact that she had every single night free was her new reality. "I'm available Monday through Thursday."

He scanned the brochures, then handed three back to her. "Let's check these first. I'd take the day off but Norm Pinkerton is out for knee surgery and he's second-in-command. I really can't take any vacation days for a few weeks."

"Evenings are fine," she assured him. "I'll make arrangements. Our local venues hunger for business in the winter. They'll offer us price concessions we'd never get in the busy season, and they'll throw in extras to tempt you to sign with them."

"I love a great deal," he admitted. "But won't that just muddy the waters?"

"Not with me on board." She filed the brochures he'd chosen into a folder and started to stand.

He beat her to it, stood and reached down a hand to help her up.

Hand in hand, he pulled her upright, then steadied her with his other hand at her waist.

Electricity buzzed. The lights might have dimmed, or flashed or maybe they did nothing at all, maybe it was just the feel of her hand wrapped in his. Warm, solid, strong, yet gentle, as if he was the kind of man who was strong enough to be gentle.

Back away. He thinks you're an airheaded beauty queen, and he's kind of a jerk, so pretend you felt nothing and do your job.

She obeyed her conscience happily. Grant McCarthy may have traveled a tough road since his wife left, but she'd been handed a similar set of walking papers from her rich, self-absorbed ex-husband, and she wasn't a jerk about it.

She slipped her hand away, pretended his touch had no effect on her and took a firm step back. "I'll set these up and let you know the details. Do you prefer phone or email contact?"

"Email's fine."

Of course it was. Why would he want any more human contact with her than absolutely necessary?

She nodded, tapped her folder and moved toward the stairs. "I'll send you times as soon as I have them."

"I'll be watching for them."

She heard Rory laugh and chat as she helped Grant get the twins' jackets fastened, and as the upstairs glass door swung silently shut behind her, she paused, wishing she could go back and help with those two priceless children.

She knew that kids with disabilities did better with high expectations. The thought that Grant McCarthy was content with babying that little girl made her pulse race.

Of course, when he'd held her hand her pulse raced in a different way, but she chalked that up to reading too many romances lately. Since coming home a year before, she'd avoided dating. She was back in Grace Haven on temporary assignment, to help her parents in a time of need. Her father was fighting brain cancer, and her mother's popular event-planning business was funding the cost of experimental treatments in Texas. To keep the business going, she and her sister Kimberly had stepped in to help.

Kimberly was a natural at wedding planning. She'd learned the business alongside their mother, and with her parents' impending retirement, it was natural for Kimberly to step into the role of running Kate & Company.

Emily was more at home on the wedding-gown end of things. Outfitting a bridal party, choosing materials and coordinating an entire look of a wedding came naturally to the former department store women's fashion buyer.

Dealing with the chronic back-and-forth of event planning drove her a little crazy. It stifled her creativity. But if it helped her father's prognosis, she could be crazy for however long it took.

But then—what next?

She had no idea, but she was pretty sure it wouldn't be here in her hometown. She didn't want to step on Kimberly's toes, or be given a job out of sympathy.

She wanted respect. The respect she'd been denied in marriage, the respect she'd been denied professionally when her ex-husband's father dismissed her from the company. Grant McCarthy's cutting remark voiced what too many felt, that pageants were nothing more than pretty girls on parade. Her titles had paid for her education, and given her inroads with top designers, but that didn't alter some opinions that pageants were nothing but fluff, and that meant the contestants were, too.

At what point would she stop feeling the need to prove herself and just be Emily?

Her parents had been proud of her pageant success, so Grant McCarthy could just stifle his negativity. She didn't need it, didn't want it and wasn't about to put up with being anyone else's castoff, ever again. Not personally and not professionally.

Chapter Two

Later that day, Grant spotted the international number code pop up on his cell phone. He grabbed the phone as he muted college football on TV. "Christa, hey! How are you? How's everything going? Isn't it the middle of the night over there?"

"I'm all right," she told him, and she sounded good. So good. "I'm on an overnight and had some time and figured the kids might be in bed."

"They are—we've got temporary peace in the kingdom." He laughed when he said it because he knew the reality behind the words. "I met with the wedding planner today, and we're scoping out reception places this week. I checked the guest list and figured about a hundred and thirty people, right?"

"The guest list. Yes. I—" A slight pause ensued, as if he'd lost the connection.

"Christa, you there?"

"Yes. Yes, I'm here." She still sounded funny, though. Almost cautious. "Yes, around one thirty with both families and friends. Maybe a few more. I'm guilt stricken that I'm sticking you with all this. It's not like your life is exactly easy, but Mrs. Gallagher is a sweetheart. She'll smooth things out for you."

"Well, it's Emily I'm working with. The middle sister." With the great hair, gorgeous face and take-no-prisoners attitude.

"Emily's back?" Surprise raised Christa's voice. "The last I knew she was married and living in Philadelphia."

"Well, she appears to be single and here in Grace Haven," Grant told her. "She and Kimberly are running the business while her father undergoes treatment."

"The cancer. Of course." Christa's voice deepened. "I've got him on my prayer list," she went on. Static messed up her next words, but Grant heard the last phrase succinctly. "I hate cancer."

"Me, too," Grant told her, though he wasn't putting stock in prayer lists. His mother had been an amazingly devout woman, and what did that get her?

Two extended bouts with cancer before they

lost her. His father had walked out on them over thirty years before, and Grant used to pray his heart out as a little kid, begging God to bring his dad back. It never happened. His prayers went unanswered, and that was a good lesson learned at a young age. God didn't exist, because if he did, he didn't take his job all that seriously. Grant took everything seriously as a result. "I'll keep you updated on things either through email or phone, okay?"

"Yes, thank you! And if you can copy Spencer, that would be great."

"Will do. And don't you worry about anything," he instructed. "Your job is to stay safe, finish this deployment and get married. Everything here will be fine, I promise."

"Thank you! I love you, Grant."

Her words made him smile. "I love you, too. We're all we've got now, so we've got to stick together."

Silence greeted his words again. When she finally answered him, he realized it must be a delayed connection. "We'll stick together, all right. Hey, gotta go. I'll call again soon, okay?"

"Yes. Goodbye, Chris—"

The phone hummed in his ear. She'd hung up.

He set his phone down and turned off the game. Life *was* somewhat crazy right now, and he didn't see that getting better anytime soon.

He had the kids in the only day care center comfortable with Dolly's behavior issues, his eccentric aunt thought he was spreading himself too thin and needed a wife, and the twins were generally either catching something or getting over something.

This was his normal.

He pulled into his aunt and uncle's yard on Monday morning, ready to start a new week. Aunt Tillie bustled out the side door to greet him while Uncle Percy followed at a less frenetic pace.

"How are the wedding plans coming?" Aunt Tillie demanded in a too-loud voice. "You makin' progress?"

He fibbed slightly. He assumed they were, but he had thought he'd hear from Emily Gallagher and he hadn't. "Yes. If I need to go check out some wedding stuff tonight, can you sit with the kids?"

"What those little ones need is a mother," Tillie declared for about the hundredth time. "I can't say it's right." She shook her head firmly, and her frown matched the motion. "Them bein' in day care all day, then with a sitter at night, but if you need me, I'll be here. Hi, darlins!" She smiled and waved into the backseat, blowing kisses a mile a minute.

The twins laughed and waved back as he

and Uncle Percy pulled out of the driveway. He dropped the kids at Mary Flanagan's day care center, got to work and as soon as his office door slapped shut behind him, he called Kate & Company. When Allison put the call through to Emily, he pretended the sound of her voice didn't make him want to suck his stomach in. He was in good shape and he didn't care what Emily Gallagher thought about anything other than weddings. "Miss Gallagher, I thought I'd hear from you by now. I was wondering if you were able to set up times for me to see those wedding venues."

"Of course." She sounded surprised, and her next words explained why. "I sent you an email Saturday afternoon confirming two stops tonight, one at five thirty and one at seven, and then tomorrow night at six for the third venue. I'm sorry you didn't get it."

"Nope, not here," he replied, but then he noticed his spam folder wasn't empty. There it was, an email from Kate & Company. "Wait, I lied. Your email got spammed."

She laughed, and he realized it was a nice laugh, soft and kind. The kind of laugh that made you feel better about things and made small children giggle out loud. Like Dolly did last week. "So are we okay for tonight?" she asked. "Do you have someone who can watch Timmy and Dolly?"

She remembered their names.

Why did that mean something?

He didn't know why, but it did because almost everyone referred to them as a set. *How are the twins? Can you bring the twins? Hey, Grant, I saw the twins yesterday...*

Hearing her call them by name sloughed off some of his gruffness. "Aunt Tillie and Uncle Percy are coming over. They'll stay as late as they need to."

"Perfect. I'll meet you at the Edgewater Inn for the first appointment at five thirty. We can go on from there."

"I'll see you then."

He went through the day going over a winter preparedness checklist with the town staff. Being ready for winter storms meant planning in advance, and as they rechecked everything from salt to backup plow blades and which roads had botched pothole patches rising above road level, his eyes strayed to the big round clock on the wall several times.

"Boss, you got an appointment?" Jeannie Delgado asked around four thirty. "Because you've had your eye on that clock the past hour."

"I do, so let's call an end to this meeting." He stood, gathered his things and pulled his jacket on. "I've got to get the kids home to Tillie. I'm meeting with the wedding planner the next two nights so we can pick things for Christa's wedding."

"Marvelous!" Jeannie's inflection offered full approval. "You're a good brother, Grant. So many folks don't bother with family these days. Having family around is a wonderful thing. Enjoy your evening and if they give out samples of cake, bring a few back here tomorrow."

"Cake is on Friday's schedule, on my lunch hour," he told her. "And I haven't even begun to figure out how Christa's going to search for a wedding gown. How do you find a wedding gown from overseas? Buy it there and ship it back?"

"I have no idea." Jeannie frowned. "Maybe she'll buy it online, have it delivered here then have it altered at the last minute?"

He'd been feeling pretty good about checking out reception spots. Food he understood, and as the man in charge of a multimillion-dollar town highway budget, he had a great head for numbers. But ribbons and lace? Flowers?

No, no, and no.

Circumstances left him little choice, so he drove to day care, picked up two busy children, dealt with Dolly's backseat anger issues for over five miles and got them home to Aunt Tillie. Then he showered and changed, got back in the car and drove to the Edgewater Inn. He arrived five minutes early, something that didn't happen often now that he was a single dad. When Emily Gallagher pulled into the lot driving a cherry-red SUV, he realized anew that this woman had spent her life being noticed and didn't mind it in the least. Just knowing that made him want— no...make that *need*—to keep a distance. He'd lived that scenario once. He had no intention of living it again.

"You made it." She smiled a welcome as he walked toward her.

"I did."

"Excellent. Now, when we get inside the new chef's name is Henry, but he likes to be called Henri, so when I do that to appease his some-what crazy artistic nature, don't laugh. Okay?"

"Well, now I'll have to laugh because you mentioned it," he admitted. "If you'd said noth-ing, I'd have simply assumed that Henri was his name."

"So I'm safer if I leave you in the dark? If I refuse to spill any insider wedding-planning secrets?"

Hints of gold brightened her brown eyes, and standing this close, he realized tiny points of ivory lightened the darkness around her pupil, giving her a winsome look that matched her bright smile.

Except he was immune to bright smiles and winsome was overrated. "I can handle secrets on a limited basis. The problem with telling me information is that I might mess up everything by blurting it out at the worst possible time."

"I consider myself forewarned." She walked to the well-lit formal entrance. He reached out to draw the door open. She had to duck under his arm to go in, and when she straightened on the other side, the dark green wool of her coat brushed his cheek.

The delicious vanilla scent made him think of country kitchens, warm fires and snow-filled nights. When she shifted to face him as they moved down the broad hall, the combination of bright eyes, gorgeous hair, soft scent and subtle lipstick made him long to draw closer.

He couldn't, but he wanted to and that was a dangerous combination. He had a job to do, two jobs, actually. Raising two kids on his own wasn't ever going to be a simple task, and running the town's highway force kept thousands of people safe every day. No way could he afford to have his attention split, but the minute they walked into the inn manager's office and Emily shrugged off her coat, he realized working with Emily for the next two months wasn't going to be a walk in the park.

His ex-wife had always said redheads should never wear pink.

She was wrong about that and a great many other things, because Emily Gallagher tossed that mane of auburn hair over the shoulder of a hot-pink dress, slipped into the upholstered chair the inn manager offered and withdrew her electronic notepad with finesse. If Chef Henri kept looking at her like that, Grant was tempted to give him a firm right jab to the chin. "Henry?"

The chef turned, obviously miffed by his pronunciation, but Grant didn't care. At least the guy stopped eyeing Emily.

"Henri." The chef's haughty manner was an instant turnoff, but the dishes they sampled were magnificent. For great food and a reasonable price, Grant could deal with Henri's arrogance if he needed to.

"This raspberry reduction with the burgundy and nut-crusted pork is amazing." Emily made a note on her tablet. "And those mushroom potatoes? Henri, I'd love to learn how to make those. I don't suppose you'd share the recipe, would you?"

Henri laughed and didn't look the least bit humble. "Henri has, of course, studied much to achieve the pinnacles of food, so no, I cannot share the chef's secrets I've acquired, but I will be happy now just knowing you approve."

The inn manager cleared his throat, as if reminding the chef that the final decision wasn't up to Emily. The chef redirected his attention to Grant with a slight huff, then waited while Grant sampled a charbroiled steak with mushroom, bread and herb stuffing. "Amazing. This is tricky enough to create for one person, much less re-creating it for over a hundred. You've outdone yourself, Henri."

His compliment must have soothed the cook's ruffled feathers because he held up a hand. "One moment." He disappeared, then reappeared with two crystal cups, filled with something warm and sweet. "A treat to sample. This is a delicious way to wrap up a crisp evening, no?"

Grant tasted his, and he was about to sing the dessert's praises when Emily sighed and held her glass aloft after one spoonful. "Perfection in a cup. The hint of caramel balances the background of cinnamon, and is that nutmeg or allspice I taste?"

Henri beamed and shrugged, ready to carry the secret to his grave.

"Nutmeg," she decided. She took another taste, then smiled again. "Clever, Henri! And delicious. What did you think, Mr. McCarthy?"

Right now having her use his full name seemed preposterous. The inn manager sent him an odd look. "Grant, please. We'll be working together for some time, so of course first names are in order."

She sent him an almost impudent look, but held her tongue. "This bread pudding, Grant." She took one more taste and languished over it, and he was pretty sure she did it on purpose. "Amazing, right?"

"One of the best desserts I've ever had, Henri. A hint of French to soften the simplicity of Old English."

Henri's smile widened. "That is exactly what I was looking for! Old, new, French, English, American blended as one."

"Henri, I know you've got other things to do this evening to get ready for tomorrow's banquet. Thank you." The inn manager motioned to a small table nearby. "If you would both sit here, I can go over the options with a pricing sheet, and then print up an actual price list for Captain McCarthy's wedding if you book with us."

By the time they'd finished, they had exactly ten minutes to get to the next appointment, a hillside vineyard and party house overlooking the southern end of the lake. Grant followed Emily there, parked next to her then accompanied her into the vineyard.

He knew it was wrong instantly. Too new, too garish, too many lights, not enough charm. When they'd finished the tasting and Emily cut them loose quickly, he knew she understood. They got to her car before she spoke. "Good call on that. First, you kept your opinion to yourself and that's a favor to me because I have to work with these folks as long as I'm here, working at Kate & Company. Thank you for being discreet."

As long as she was here? He leaned one hand against her car. "You're welcome. I do have manners most of the time," he told her. "What do you mean, as long as you're here? Are you leaving?" he asked. "The correct answer would be no, because if you leave in the middle of these wedding plans, I'm toast."

"I'll be here to see Christa's wedding through." She opened the back door and tucked her notebook inside her bag before she turned back.

"But you're not staying here? In Grace Haven?" It shouldn't surprise him. Emily had big city written all over her.

She met his gaze frankly. "There aren't a lot of jobs for clothing buyers in Grace Haven."

He frowned. "But you have a job with Kate & Company."

"Currently, yes. But once Dad's on the mend, I think Kimberly can handle this with one hand tied behind her back. She's an absolute whiz with event planning. My guess is she won't need her little sister hanging around." She tipped her gaze up to the crystal clear sky, then sighed with appreciation. "Doesn't looking up at the vastness of the night sky just fill you with wonder? You don't get views like this in the city."

It didn't fill him with wonder because he was too busy looking down, but he followed her gaze to the pinpoints of galactic sparkle and agreed. "Amazing."

"Wondrous, right? Anyway." She shrugged lightly. "Taking over Mom's business is perfect for Kimberly. She's spent her life grooming herself for this, and I'm not about to step on her toes. But in the meantime, I'm here to help so that Mom and Dad have no worries. Living at home gives me zero expenses, so I can plan my next steps. If I end up in a big city, the cost of living gets absolutely crazy."

"I see." He'd lived life with a discontented woman once. He'd dealt with the result, too, and he wasn't about to take that risk again. "Well, I'm glad you're here to guide me through the whole process."

"Me, too." The sincerity of her tone warmed him, and once again he was drawn, but she'd just cemented reasons to resist the attraction. He was staying. She was leaving. End of story.

"Tomorrow we'll stop at the Lodge at Fairhaven. They're new, but they do a great job."

"That's where my cousin's wedding was, wasn't it?"

"You don't remember?" She made a face as he swung her car door open. "It couldn't have been all that good if you don't remember it from last spring."

"Dolly was sick." He shrugged. "When you're doing this stuff on your own and you get a sick kid, you opt out of the party and stay home."

"My dad was like that, too. All about priorities."

"Your father's a good guy." Grant lowered his voice, unsure how to approach the next subject. "I'm glad he's doing better, but I was sorry to hear about the cancer. I lost my mom to breast cancer and I wasn't ready to say goodbye."

"Are we ever?" She stared up at the stars once more, then looked back at him. Her breath puffed a tiny cloud of frozen steam into the air until a breath of wind sent it dancing away. "I'm sorry you lost her. Is your dad still alive?"

"Don't know. Don't much care. He left when Christa was a baby. I barely remember him, so it's like I never had a father. My mother never remarried—she said it was too risky with me and my sister. What if she married the wrong person? What if he was mean to us? So she wouldn't let herself date or get interested in anyone until we were on our own, and by that time, she'd already had her first bout of cancer. She survived that one, but the second round, well..." He waited a moment to let the rise of emotion pass. "You know."

"So being a good father is truly important to you."

He stuffed his hands into his jacket pockets and gave a slow nod. "Yeah, of course. I didn't have one so it's not like I've got some great role model, but my mother was solid. I kind of do what she would have done except I'm more cautious, I don't bake cookies and I'm a lousy cook. Happily, Dolly and Tim love PB&J, mac and cheese, and Oreos. With the occasional vegetable thrown in as long as it's corn or squash."

"They're beautiful kids."

They were, and because he was their only parent, he needed to have a plan, always. "Thank you. I'm real lucky to have them."

She flashed him a look he couldn't read, then nodded. "Kids are a blessing, for sure. Well." She slipped into her car. "I'll see you tomorrow, then."

He didn't want to wait until tomorrow, but he wasn't a rash man. He didn't act on impulse. He couldn't afford to, not now when two small children meant so much. He wasn't about to make foolish mistakes to disrupt their lives. He stepped back, lifted his hand and nodded. "See you then."

If ever a man needed some serious roadside repair, it was Grant McCarthy. Oh, she saw the good side of the guy. His devotion to his children, his strong work ethic, the sacrificial nature and his strong, rugged good looks. A man who saw what needed to be done and simply did it. Those were all wonderful qualities.

But Emily had learned one thing during her years of pageants and contests. Judging was fine on stage, but in everyday life, judgmental people weren't her style and the minute Grant McCarthy started talking about his father, red flags popped up.

Judge not, that ye be not judged.

She'd lived both sides of that wise verse. She was older now and wiser than the college-age contestant she'd been when Chris Barrister won her heart six years ago.

He'd tossed her aside when he grew tired of her, and she'd learned to be more cautious as a result. No one would ever get to treat her or her heart casually ever again.

But something about Grant spoke to her.

Was it because they'd both suffered through rough marriages? His wife dumped him. Her husband gave her the boot, albeit with a generous settlement, but the buyout didn't heal the ache of knowing she wasn't enough. No matter how hard she worked, how sweet or funny or kind she was, how good she looked, she hadn't been enough to keep him happy for more than two years of marriage. Being let go from his father's company simply underscored rampant opinion that she'd gotten the job through nothing more than looking good and being married to the boss's son.

That galled her because she'd done a great job for Barrister's, Inc., and the women's department sales figures had increased dramatically while she sat in the head buyer's chair. She'd garnered recognition and job interest from other department store chains when Noel Barrister let her go, but then Dad got sick and she knew what she needed to do.

So here she was, in Grace Haven, following in Kimberly's shadow once again.

She pulled into the driveway a few minutes later, drove past the carriage house garage, where her future brother-in-law and his daughter, Amy, lived, and walked into her parents' house, restless.

"How'd it go?" Kimberly looked up from her

laptop. "Did he pick a venue tonight or are you still on for tomorrow night?"

"Tomorrow night," Emily said. She flopped down into her father's favorite recliner, kicked off her shoes and rubbed her sore, aching feet. "Remind me to get rid of those shoes, no matter how nice they look with this dress."

"That dress is a knockout," Rory said as she came in from the kitchen. She took one look at Emily, then sank onto the carpet and started rubbing her sister's feet. "What's wrong? Did tonight go badly?"

"No. It was fine. I'm just—" Emily thought, came up with nothing and shrugged. "Out of sorts. Restless. Wondering about everything, the meaning of life, why things happen like they do and why women feel the need to wear stupid shoes."

"You like him," Kimberly noted from her chair.

It was beyond annoying to have an older sister who prided herself on being right, especially when it was true too much of the time. "At this moment I don't like anyone."

"Mmm-hmm." Kimberly jotted something into the laptop, and said, "Invite him to my wedding."

"Not gonna happen." She looked down at

Rory, still massaging the ache out of her left foot. "Thank you."

A big *woof* sounded from outside.

Mags had been sound asleep, curled in a tiny ball on the carpet, but when Drew Slade's German shepherd barked, she sprang up, raced to the door and stood on her tiny back legs, pawing.

"Come on, Mags." Drew came through the door, let the little dog out then slid the door shut. "Cold and getting colder. They said snow in the mountains."

"And so it begins." Emily lolled her head back and waved to him. "Hey, Drew."

He smiled at her, winked and walked across the floor to Kimberly. "You can tell it's a sure thing when your future wife doesn't even bother to get out of her chair to greet you with a kiss."

Kimberly hit one last button, set the computer aside and gave him the kiss he sought.

Emily pouted inside.

She had thought she'd had that once. What was it that made someone fickle? To want something else, someone else? Was it her lack or his selfishness? Or both? Or had she fallen for the glitz of the whole thing? There were many questions and not enough answers.

"Hey." Rory squeezed her foot as Drew and

Kimberly moved into the kitchen to find food and discuss their upcoming wedding. And probably kiss more. "Don't look back. Gaze forward. Remember that awesome Einstein quote?"

She made a face and Rory laughed. "There are only two ways to live. One is as if nothing is a miracle. The other is as if everything is."

"Perspective."

"Yup." Rory switched feet. "With Dad's problems, I have to push myself to remember we've had him all our lives. How blessed we were to have both parents, a home, heat, clothing."

"You're so much better than I am," Emily remarked. "Take my feet, for example. If you'd come in with sore feet, I'd have said 'Wow, go soak in a tub. That'll help.'"

Rory smiled up at her. "So does this."

"You make things personal. Maybe that's part of my problem. Maybe I don't make things personal."

Rory sighed and gave her foot a smack.

"Hey!"

"You don't have a problem. You're a wonderful person. The worst thing you did was fall in love with the wrong person because he pretended he was the right person."

"You're letting me off too easy," Emily replied and when Rory started to argue, she held up a hand. "I was kind of young and shallow,

Rory. I can own it now. When Christopher started courting me I was at the top of my game. I'd been Miss New York, I aced college, I was ready to move on to the next perfect step. Marrying a rich guy, falling into an amazing job as a department store buyer and living in a mansion made me feel like a princess. I liked it. So I can't lay all the blame at his feet."

"Lots of girls want to be princesses," Rory told her.

"But not you. Never you. Why?"

Rory shrugged. "Not my thing. I'm not the gilded type, I guess. But in spite of why you came home last year, I'm glad you did. Handling Dad's illness is a whole lot easier for me when we're all in this together." She stood up and kissed Emily's cheek. "I'm subbing tomorrow in a first grade classroom, so I'm heading up to bed. Good night, Em."

"Good night."

The murmur of voices in the kitchen told her Drew and Kimberly were deep in discussion. She was just about to go to bed herself when her phone buzzed. She pulled up a text from Grant and sighed. He'd sent her a picture of Timmy and Dolly, sleeping, tangled in covers, sharing a bed. And under it Grant had typed, Unusual moment of peace, now recorded for posterity.

Something sweet and gentle curled inside her. She sent back a single-word reply. Precious.

She went to bed, smiling, the image of those two sweet children blending with Einstein's words.

Chapter Three

"Well, don't you look handsome," Aunt Tillie remarked the next evening. "Percy, don't Grant look handsome tonight?"

Uncle Percy grunted, unimpressed, but when Timmy saw him dressed in a turtleneck and a sport coat, he frowned. "I go bye-bye, too."

"Not this time, little man. Daddy's got to go see more people about Auntie's wedding."

His words didn't impress the toddler. "I go bye-bye wif Daddy."

Grant squatted down, hugged the toddler and shook his head. "No can do, Daddy's got some things he has to do. Aunt Tillie and Uncle Percy are with you tonight."

"I go!" Dolly crawled across the dining area, grabbed a kitchen chair leg, hauled herself up and stomped a foot. "I go!"

"Not you, either, button. And on that note…"

He gave Dolly a kiss, kissed Timmy again and left his aunt with two squalling children. "Sorry."

She waved him off, calm as ever. "This is all for your benefit, Grant. They'll be fine in two minutes. You'll feel guilty all night while they play and laugh and giggle and eat mac and cheese. Go, get this done, and Christa will be thrilled."

He walked to the garage, torn. He'd gotten a lecture today from Dolly's occupational therapist, reminding him that she needed to work on skills daily, but that was easier said than done. Dolly had become an expert at refusing to do the simplest tasks, which meant her motor skills were dragging even further behind.

Was Aunt Tillie right? Were they really fine in a couple of minutes while he wore a mantle of guilt all evening? He drove to the lodge, saw Emily's SUV then felt guilty for looking forward to the evening. He got out, crossed the couple of spaces to her car and opened the door for her.

"Thank you!" Her bright smile warmed him, and that only made the guilt mount higher. "How was your day?"

His day had been fine until fifteen minutes ago, and he didn't want to lay all that at her door, so he shrugged. "It was okay. Yours?"

She studied him, then shook her head. "You're worried about something. If it has to do with the wedding, spill it now."

"It's not about the wedding." And then, ten seconds after deciding not to lay it at her door, he recounted the kids' antics. She nodded, frowned in sympathy then laughed out loud.

He tucked his neck deeper in his coat, aggrieved. "It wasn't one bit funny when two little kids were crying because they miss their daddy and I'm too busy to be with them."

"It is kind of funny," she insisted. "Because Tillie is right. I told you I worked in a children's home during college, and this is textbook toddler attachment stuff. We even started messaging pics to the parents five minutes later to prove our point. They're fine, they're just experts at pushing the guilt button. They don't like the moment of separation, and boy, do they let you know it. I bet if Aunt Tillie was to send you a picture right now, it would be of two happy, healthy, goofy kids playing or eating and having the time of their lives."

"Which is exactly what they say at day care, too." He worked his jaw, then shrugged one shoulder. "I'm a pushover when it comes to them."

She moved forward to the lodge door, let him

open it and smiled over her shoulder. "Tell me something I don't know."

He let the door swing shut behind them and followed her to the hostess station.

He liked the setting instantly. One part of the lodge was a restaurant, known for great food and its cozy, rustic atmosphere. Cozy and rustic worked for him, and he was pretty sure it would work for two air force officers tying the knot.

When the owner/manager sat down with them and covered everything in detail, Grant was sold, unless the food tasting went bad.

It didn't.

Instead of the tiny bites he'd been offered last night, the lodge owner served them a full meal at a linen-draped table complete with a centerpiece and a candle, alongside a fireplace.

It was like a date, only it wasn't, he reminded himself.

But the feeling persisted as they laughed and talked their way through dinner. "This is amazing," he told her.

"The Celtic stew, the homemade bread or the beef?"

"All of it, plus the setting, the service and the prices are so reasonable. And I like the idea of family-style dining."

"Dishes at the table, everybody sharing. I like

that, too. It's Sunday-dinner-friendly and most folks enjoy that."

"The phrase *pass the peas* becomes a conversation starter."

"Exactly." She smiled at him, made a note in her tablet and sipped her water.

"I bet Timmy and Dolly would love the big animals on the walls." She pointed over his shoulder to the authentic-looking deer, moose and bear.

He winced. "They're two. Taking them out to eat usually turns into a food fight. Timmy's getting a little better, but Dolly's stubbornness gets in the way, so we rarely go anyplace." He waited, and when she said nothing, he nodded an acknowledgment. "Of course, it's pretty clear she's got me somewhat snowed."

"Somewhat," Emily agreed, but she said it gently, as if she didn't want to hurt his feelings. Grant appreciated that. Between Tillie, the occupational therapist and day care, everyone had something to say these days. That meant they were probably correct, but he appreciated Emily's gentler approach.

"So tonight, we need to have coffee or something," she told him outside. "We can go to the diner, but it's late and they'll be closing. Or we can sit down at your place or mine. Rory stopped by Gabriella's bakery today."

"If we go to my place and wake the kids, we'll get nothing done, so if you don't mind, your place sounds good. And the baked goods seal the deal."

"I'll meet you there."

Emily parked her car behind Kimberly's and waited until Grant pulled in alongside her. She climbed out and headed to the walk, waiting. He took longer than she expected, and when a blast of eastbound wind tunneled in from the west, she pulled her coat tighter. He glanced her way, looking surprised.

Realization flashed in his eyes. He popped the door open and pocketed his phone, looking contrite. "Sorry. I wanted to give Tillie an idea of my time frame, but you didn't have to wait. It's cold out here."

She started for the door. "I didn't want you to feel awkward coming in."

"Do you make people feel awkward?"

She turned to face him and caught his smile beneath the lamps lighting the stoned path. "I try not to. Guess my success rate could use an upgrade."

"My batting average isn't all it could be, either," he told her, and the way he said it sounded like he understood regret.

"We usually have meetings in the office." She

indicated The Square up the road. "But there's no sense going over there, turning on all the lights when there are perfectly delicious cookies and brownies here, courtesy of my sister Rory." She opened the door as she mentioned Rory's name, and her sister waved from the far side of the living room.

"Grant?"

Kimberly came through from the kitchen. So did Drew. "I'm Kimberly. I haven't had the pleasure of meeting you yet, but Dad says a lot of good stuff about you."

"When the highway department can keep the old police chief and the new police chief's office happy, then everybody's happy," Grant told her. He nodded toward Drew, the newly appointed chief of police. "This guy's got some pretty big shoes to fill, because your father did one solid job as chief. But so far, so good." He winked at Drew as he shook Kimberly's hand.

"Feeling's mutual." Drew clapped him on the back. "You did a great job facilitating that meeting of the town leaders the other day. I appreciated it."

"I forgot that you two will actually have to work together on some things now." Emily made a face. "My bad."

"Grant, I know this is short notice, but if you can sneak away for a few hours next week, come to our wedding." Drew took a seat at the big round oak table and motioned Grant to sit down. "We've got plenty of room and food. We'd love to have you there."

Grant grimaced. "I'd like to, but I'm walking around with way too much guilt for leaving Tim and Dolly as much as I do already. It seems like I'm not home nearly as much as I'd like to be."

"Bring them along," Kimberly said. Grant gave her a blank stare.

"You didn't just say that. Did you?"

"I did, and I meant it. It's not a huge affair. We actually like kids, and I'd rather have you come and bring the kids than not come," Kimberly told him. "Call it good town relations or whatever, but I think the kids will have fun, there will be all kinds of people there to spoil them and how can that be a bad thing?"

It wasn't a bad thing, but Grant's hesitation indicated he might not agree.

"I know they're little," Emily offered. "And they probably get overwhelmed easily, but if you'd like to bring them, there's a whole crew of Gallaghers who will be happy to help with them."

"Dolly actually has a bunch of cute dresses she's never worn because we don't do fancy all that often," he admitted.

"Nothing like a wedding to put on the dog,"

Drew drawled, as if getting dressed up for anything—even his own wedding—was cruel and unusual punishment.

"Think about it." Kimberly reached out a hand to Drew and tugged. "I expect you and Emily have things to talk about, so I'm going to drag my fiancé out to the front room and we're going to give the to-do list one last look."

"It's beyond crazy how even a small family wedding can need this much attention." Rory tipped her glasses down and peered up at Kimberly from her spot across the room. "Although in this case it might be because we have experts running their own show."

"Hush." Kimberly leaned down and gazed hard into Rory's laughing eyes. "You don't want to bite the hand that feeds you. And this is a somewhat important day in my life, brat."

"Good point."

Rory grinned and ducked back to her laptop, while Emily pulled her chair a little closer to Grant's and brought up the online contracts. "I know you need to get home, so if we can go over the major points here, I'll print things up and we're good to go. Unless you'd rather have me email it to you so you can examine the details back at your place."

"Here's good. Ditches and roads are my forte,

not party planning. Which is why I came to the best."

When he said it, he looked straight at Emily, as if assured she could do the job without her mother or big sister looking over her shoulder. His vote of confidence felt good, if a bit surprising after his initial reaction to her. "I'll contact Christa about the other things. Dress, attendants, flowers. Whatever else she has in mind, I'll be happy to run interference for her."

"You don't mind?"

"Not in the least. That's my favorite part of the process." She tapped a few keys as she spoke, filled in a few more spots and hit Print. "I'm happy to do it. Let's not forget that Kate & Company managed to put together a star-studded wedding for the president's daughter, while her whole family was stomping the campaign trail two months ago. Ninety percent of that was in absentia."

"And it was amazing," Drew called from the other room. "Not that I'm listening to you guys or anything."

Drew's words seemed to bolster Grant. "If you could talk to Christa, and make everything flow for her, I don't think there's enough money in the world to show my thanks. She asked me to stand with her, so that's a little weird already."

"As her witness? What a perfectly lovely

thing to do, brother and sister, standing before God together."

He made a face. "I'd have been okay with just walking the bride down the aisle and maintaining a low profile for the remainder of the day."

"That makes Christa's gesture sweeter." She handed him the hard-copy contract. "I've got Christa's email now. Maybe she and I can arrange a Skype session at the bridal salon. And with so many possibilities online, we can come up with something absolutely beautiful for her."

Grant withdrew his phone and pulled up a picture of a happy couple with snow-capped mountains in the background. "This was taken two years ago when they were at a ski lodge in Colorado. She's built like you," he told Emily. "But taller. She usually likes things kind of simple, but that's everyday stuff." He frowned at the picture. "When it comes to a wedding gown, who knows?"

"It's always the ones you least expect who choose a princess gown," Rory muttered as she closed her laptop and stood. "And the princesses pick a mermaid dress and can't climb into the overpriced limo without help."

"Yeah, like that," Grant agreed. He shifted to face Emily directly again. "You don't mind doing that part, too?"

"I'll love it. I'll get hold of Christa as soon

as I can. We'll set something up and I'll keep you in the loop."

Rory had crossed to the kitchen. She came back and set a tray of pastries in front of Grant. "Gabby sent these as a thank-you for the business we've been bringing her, and Kimberly made it abundantly clear that they need to disappear," she instructed. "Something about fitting into that wedding gown next week."

"Let's send a few home with him," Emily suggested. "Leave a couple for Amy, but if we send them with Grant, the twins will be beside themselves, and Tillie and Percy will love us forever."

"Percy's got a sweet tooth, for certain, but—"

Emily stepped closer, reaching one hand up, over his mouth. She slid her gaze toward the living room, then raised one brow. "Taking them will be an act of kindness, Grant. There's a bride in the next room," she whispered. "Save her from herself, and just take the pastries. Okay?"

His eyes met hers, and this time they didn't stray. They lingered and twinkled as if he liked looking into her eyes. "Okay."

Her heart fluttered. She moved her hand away from his face, but couldn't draw her eyes from his.

"I'll just put these on a double paper plate, Grant." Rory's movement broke the moment, and maybe Emily was wrong. Maybe it wasn't even a moment.

But when she walked Grant to the door, he turned and held her gaze once more. Then he reached out and took her hand while raising the plate of treats. "The family will love these. Thank you."

He squeezed her hand lightly and smiled.

Gone was the defensiveness she'd seen last week. In its place was an easy grin. She smiled back, and when he released her hand, her fingers felt downright cold and lonely as she closed the door.

She couldn't get involved, she knew that, but for that brief moment, getting involved felt like an absolutely wonderful thing to do.

Chapter Four

He shared the pastries with Tillie and Percy when he got home. The twins were in bed, and all was well.

It actually *wasn't* well, but Grant didn't know that until he went to check on the toddlers. Timmy had climbed out of bed and was sleeping on the floor of his room. Grant opened the door, bumped it into the sleeping boy and pinched his little fingers between the door and the floor.

The toddler woke with a start, shrieking in surprise and pain.

Dolly woke up in the adjacent room, not because she was in pain, but because Timmy was upset. She burst into tears of sympathy, or possibly envy because now Timmy was in Grant's arms, garnering all the attention.

"I'm sorry. I'm sorry, Timmers." He kissed

the boy's hand, put ice on the fingers, then kissed it again when Timmy slapped the cold compress aside. "Daddy didn't mean it. I'm so sorry."

Timmy hiccupped and sobbed against his chest, but fell back asleep in quick minutes.

Not Dolly. Now that she was awake, her sixty-minute catnap offered a new lease on life. He rocked her, read to her, played with her and finally—with the clock edging toward midnight—got her back into her crib.

He crawled into bed shortly thereafter, only to have his phone alert wake him at two forty-five. He pried his eyes open, scanned the report and dispatched five truck drivers to salt the highways before people woke up and discovered nearly a quarter inch of freezing rain had fallen between midnight and two o'clock.

He couldn't sleep with workers dispatched. He sat down at his laptop and prepared to get some work done.

No internet.

He sank back into the chair, ready to punch something.

How was he supposed to do it all? How was he supposed to manage everything? His mother had worked full-time cleaning patient rooms at the local hospital, then she'd spent Saturdays housecleaning for two local families, earning just enough to make ends meet. And she hadn't gone ballistic or berserk or anything else. She'd just done it.

Why couldn't he manage that well? It wasn't rocket science; it was running a house. Caring for kids. Keeping a job. Despite his best efforts, he seemed to mess up more than most.

He laid his head against the chair back, wishing he was a better father. A better brother. A better son.

The next thing he knew, Tim was at his feet. "Daddy! Up pees, Daddy! Up, pees!"

"Hey, you're up and out of your bed again, my man. You don't smell that great." He bumped foreheads with the little guy. "Good morning."

"Mornin'!" Timmy gave him an ear-to-ear grin and patted his face. "I have toast, 'kay?"

"It's very okay. High chair or big boy chair?"

Timmy patted his chest, kind of like Tarzan. "Big boy!"

"Don't run around with your toast, okay?"

"Don't run, don't run, don't run!" He shook his finger in a perfect and tiny imitation of Aunt Tillie.

"Now if you'd only follow your own directions," Grant teased. He heard Dolly screech from upstairs. "I'll be right back. I'm going to get your sister."

"Dowwy!"

"That would be her." He brought Dolly down, changed diapers, fed them, bundled them and got out the door on time, but when he got to the end of the driveway, a thin blanket of ice still covered his rural two-lane road. He stared in disbelief, hit his Bluetooth connection and called the office. "Jeannie, I've still got ice on the road. What's going on?"

"Boss, no one got dispatched until Hank got here at five a.m. to open the service bays. Did you do a callout?"

"Yes, at two forty-five. I sent word to all five guys." He paused and scanned his phone, and there it was, an alert that said his message hadn't been sent. And he'd fallen asleep without checking.

"Jeannie, my bad. The message is here, but never got delivered. Is everyone on the road now?"

"Yes, but you've got messages from the mayor, the police chief and the county sheriff's office wondering what happened."

Shame bit deep.

He never goofed up a job. He double-checked everything to the point of being absurd, but this time he'd messed up. He didn't want to ask this next question, but he had to and the onus was all on him. "Any accidents?"

"None reported."

He breathed a sigh of relief.

"Hank called the guys in stat and they hit the road by five thirty, just enough time for most everything to melt before things got too busy."

Dolly squawked at the inactivity. To Dolly, being in the car meant the car should be moving. Sitting at the edge of the road didn't win the toddler's favor. "I'll drop the kids off and be right there."

"See you then, boss."

Guilt grabbed hold tight.

He'd created a dangerous situation today. People could have been hurt, and all because he was tired and dozed off without following up.

Nothing happened, and you'll know better next time. Everyone makes mistakes, Grant.

His mother's words came back to him, but Grant hated mistakes. He took pride in his work, and in the work of his people.

He called the sheriff, the mayor and saved Drew Slade for last. "Drew, it's Grant. I'm calling to apologize. My dispatch never got sent and I didn't realize it. This is totally on me."

"I blame the napoleons," Drew replied. "And wedding planning. And staying up too late talking to pretty girls. I appreciate the call. We're good. But you got home early comparatively, whereas I actually was up late, talking to a pretty girl."

Grant peeked into the rearview mirror. Dolly was rolling something around between her fingers, and appeared fascinated by it. He didn't need to know the object's origin; he was just glad to have her quiet for the moment. "Me, too. Mine is two years old with uneven pigtails."

"I remember those days," Drew sympathized. "I raised Amy on my own for eight years, so I hear you. It's tough, and you've got twice the workload and they're at a crazy age. It'll get better in about two years, but that's faint comfort now."

It sure was, because how was Grant going to manage those two years if he could barely manage today? He circled around the white clapboard church on Maple and pulled into the day care parking lot. "Gotta go."

"Me, too."

He removed Dolly from her seat first because Tim had the patience to wait the extra thirty seconds. When he set Dolly down to unfasten a stubborn buckle on Tim's seat, she yelled in anger and stomped her feet.

He stared at her.

She stomped them again, one after the other, angry and demanding.

Dolly's repeated action brought Emily's words to life. *Walking's always good.*

If Dolly could stomp her feet back and forth,

then she could walk. That made him look at her more carefully.

He scooped Dolly up and took Timmy's hand, to guide him up the walk. Mrs. Flanagan was waiting for them inside the door. She gave the kids a warm greeting, then settled Dolly on her hip. Grant kissed her goodbye. She flailed and yelled, reaching for him, sobbing...

"Remember what I said." Mary offered him a wise look. "She's fine five minutes after you walk out that door. Sometimes less than that, Grant."

He'd always doubted that before, figuring it was Mary's way of trying to ease the separation.

But right now, he had a deeper confidence that Mary was truly right.

His beautiful, charming and challenged daughter was a brat.

Now what was he going to do about it?

Emily spotted Grant inside the bakery, talking to Gabby and her daughter Rachel. Rachel burst out laughing at something Grant said, and when she did, she laid her hand on his sleeve...

Emily had the sudden urge to march across that room and push that hand away from Grant's water-resistant jacket.

She didn't, of course, but she wanted to, which meant the tall, brown-haired, hassled single father had gotten beneath her defenses. Based on her instantaneous reaction, she needed more than a mental list to keep the attraction at bay. She'd write a physical list that evening and post it on her mirror so she'd have a firm visual of why she should shy away from tall, handsome, rugged guys who had issues with her past.

"Emily." Gabby waved her in, excited, and Rachel met her halfway.

"We've got some amazing things for you guys to taste, Em. And I am all over that coat!" Rachel admired the waist-length bolero-style jacket with a sigh. "I can't afford it, but I'm more than slightly envious."

"It's a leftover from my buyer days," Emily told her, then slipped the short coat off and handed it over. "Try it—see what you think."

Rachel looked mortified. "No, I couldn't, I shouldn't have said anything. Mom will kill me for embarrassing her. And myself," she admitted, sheepishly.

"Rach, the one thing I walked away from Barrister's with was way too many clothes, and it's silly not to share. We're the same size. You should come over tomorrow and go through my closets. Noon, my house, bring doughnuts."

Gabby cleared her throat, which meant they should get busy, and she was right. Emily reached out to shake Grant's hand. "Hey, you got here early. The lure of cake, right? It does that to me all the time."

He'd like to say it was just the sweets that brought him to Gabby's ten minutes before their meeting time, but he'd be lying. He shook her hand, smiled and found himself in a fine mess because now that he had her hand, he really didn't want to let go.

But he did let go. "Gotta love cake."

Color climbed her cheeks, and Grant was pretty sure it wasn't from today's narrow sun or brisk wind. Or maybe he just hoped it was the effect he had on her. He reached over and pulled out a chair so Emily could sit down.

The color deepened slightly, and she smiled up at him. And that made him want to do more nice things, which was crazy absurd because hadn't she just admitted to owning closets full of clothes?

He'd done the fashion princess gig once, and the ache in his heart and his wallet had long-term effects. Emily was nice, she was runway-ready gorgeous and her laugh made him want to smile, then keep on smiling. But attraction only went so far, and he hadn't just been toasted by a beautiful woman, he'd been burned to a crisp. No way was he going to set himself up for the exact same scenario—a woman looking to move up and on.

Gabby brought a tray out of the nearby cooler. Rachel ran the counter for regular customers while Grant and Emily sampled the selection of cake squares. With a list of Christa's preferences, they made short work of ordering a small tiered cake for the wedding party and sheet cakes to be cut for the guests.

"It's really all right to do that?" Grant asked. "People won't think it's strange?"

"It's fine and sensible." She made a little face of disbelief. "I'm all about saving you money where we can. If you come in under budget, then you can give Christa and Spencer the rest of the fund, right?"

"Yes."

"So if you throw them a lovely wedding and save a couple thousand dollars, that's never a bad thing."

They set up the order with Gabby and as they left, Rachel handed Emily the jacket. Emily laughed and shook her head. "No, I was serious, and I expect to see you at noon tomorrow, rummaging my closets. And don't forget the doughnuts."

"But it's cold out."

Emily shrugged that off. "I've got a block to walk to the office. Trust me, I won't freeze."

"I'll drive you."

Grant's deep voice sent shivers up her arms that had nothing to do with the mid-November temperatures and everything to do with him. She peeked up and his gaze warmed her. "I can walk. Really."

"I've got a lot riding on this wedding," he said firmly, "and neither one of us can afford for you to get sick."

"I see. You have a vested interest in my well-being. Totally understandable."

He held the door open and followed Emily to his SUV parked just outside the bakery door. He opened the door for her, and she tried to remember the last time a man did that and came up absolutely blank.

"The heat in this thing's a bear, so you'll warm up quick," he promised as he turned the key. "That was a nice thing you did in there."

"Ordering cake?"

"The jacket."

She waved that off. "It was no biggie, honestly. I never thought of having Rachel come by and go through the bounty."

"Bounty?"

"The remains and advantages of being a major buyer and the wife of a department store chain mogul. As long as I never gain more than seven pounds, I have clothes for life."

"A dream come true."

His crisp tone made Emily's back stiffen. "I wouldn't call a broken marriage, a divorce and being dismissed from the job I loved a dream come true, but maybe it looks different from the outside." He'd pulled around the back of The Square, near the rear entrance of Kate & Company. "Thanks for the ride, Grant." She got out, grabbed her purse and electronic tablet, and paused. "I'll be in touch."

Did she slam the car door? Possibly, but then the guy deserved a wake-up call. Life wasn't about clothes, or pageant wins, or being noticed. It was about doing your best, trying your hardest, setting lofty goals and then putting in the work to achieve them.

Grant saw what he wanted to see, and he wasn't alone in his opinion. Pretty equated easy life in a lot of people's eyes, but never again would she let others rule her choices or damage her self-image.

She'd trusted once, unwisely.

One foolhardy mistake was all any girl needed.

Chapter Five

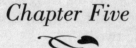

He'd messed up.

He'd insulted her with his cryptic words, and the look of pain on her face made him wish the words back. Too late.

"Grant, are you all right?" Jeannie asked that afternoon. "Did the cake put you into a sugar coma? Because you're never this quiet."

He brushed off her concern. "I'm fine, just caught up in planning winter expenses. You know that's never fun."

"But then every now and again we get a light winter and we all ease back a bit." Jeannie reached out to answer an incoming call. "I think we could all use a soft winter this year."

Wanting one and getting one were two different things. And every time he thought he had a handle on work, the phone mocked him. He'd wanted to talk to Emily about Dolly and see if she had any ideas about changing the little girl's behavior. It might not be her area of expertise, but if she'd worked with challenged youngsters for four years, that put her light-years ahead of him. He reached for the phone at the exact moment it rang beneath his fingers. Jeannie picked up the call, then said, "Grant, Emily Gallagher for you on line two."

For a thin second he hoped she was thinking of him, just like he'd been doing of her, but then he remembered the hurt look in her eyes, the look *he* put there... He ground his back teeth, then answered the phone. "Grant McCarthy."

"Grant, it's Emily."

"Three hours ago I thought I'd never want to taste cake again, but right about now I'm craving some more of Gabby's spice cake. How about you?"

She laughed, and didn't sound hurt or angry, but that was probably because she understood how to take care of a paying customer. Even the jerks. "It's amazing, isn't it? I'm calling because I just got an email from Caroline's Bridal over on Hart Street. She's doing a one-day special of free gowns for military brides a week from Tuesday. If you and I could meet there, maybe we could pick out a dress that Christa would like, or at least narrow it down. If we could set up a Skype with her, that would be great, but even if we can't, we could possibly help her get a free gown."

"They're giving them away? There's got to be a catch," Grant said, because nothing was ever really free.

"It's a national program and Caroline signed up for it, and we happen to be planning Christa's wedding at the right time. Can you manufacture some time that day? I'll contact Christa about Skyping with us and see what time would work best for her, and maybe we could plan around that."

"Yes, of course." A sudden thought made him hesitate. "This isn't like a poverty program, is it, Emily? Because we're on a budget, but we're not broke."

"It's nothing of the kind," she promised. "People across the country are contributing to show their thanks. Caroline's Bridal wanted to be part of the national appreciation effort. Pretty cool, right?"

"I'll say. Okay, you email Christa and I'll open up whatever time we need that day. Do they have evening hours in case we get a storm and I'm tied up?"

"Open until eight, so sure, we could use that

as backup, but that's the middle of the night for Christa. So—"

She was going to end the call. It was now or never. "Emily, wait. Don't hang up."

"No?"

He breathed deep. "Not yet."

"Okay. What's up?"

"Dolly." He paused, then waded in. "I've been thinking about what you said when we first met, about challenging her more."

"You mean when you got huffy with me and almost walked out? That conversation?"

"That would be the one."

"So, what's to discuss?" She sounded matter-of-fact, like the skilled businesswoman she was. "People make decisions about children all the time, and I'm not an expert, Grant. And you're not exactly open to suggestion, so maybe we should leave it at that. There are plenty of well-written books out there about raising developmentally delayed kids. That way you don't get mad at me, a plan I favor highly since we'll be working together for the next two months."

"If I promise not to get mad, act like a jerk or get defensive, do you think we could get together and talk about it?"

"Can you *do* that?" she asked, which made him laugh because she was kind of right.

"I can try," he said. "But can we do it at my house? I feel terrible leaving them so often."

"Lesson one," she murmured. "Excise guilt factor."

"You get points for recognizing that—I think it's intrinsic to single parents."

"My sister-in-law Corinne would agree. So would Drew. It's hard to be the bad guy all of the time."

"Exactly. But I don't want to raise a couple of angry, bratty kids, and if Dolly keeps demanding more and more attention, how will Timmy feel?" Something he said must have tipped her into saying yes.

"What about tomorrow? Rachel's coming over around noon, but maybe later? Or we could meet Sunday after church. That might be better. It's earlier in the day, before nap time."

"What time do you go to church?"

"Nine. And I'm home by ten thirty, so I could be at your place by eleven or so. Unless that interrupts your morning?"

"Eleven's good. I'll grab some stuff for lunch, okay?"

"No cold cuts."

Grant paused. "You don't eat cold cuts?"

"Not as a rule."

"Are you a vegetarian? Or one of those vegans?"

"No, I eat lots of things, but I don't do cold

cuts. Although I do like sliced ham. Sliced ham doesn't count."

"I'm confused. Is it a certain type you don't like or just cold cuts in general? Because that might be considered weird for a meat eater."

"I'm not weird. I'm...possibly traumatized."

He didn't mean to laugh because what if she wasn't kidding? He'd already ticked her off once today. "Trauma by luncheon meat. That's a new one, Emily. Do ninja salamis chase you in your dreams?"

She huffed, and he wondered if she was sitting at her desk, tapping a pencil against her mouth the way she did at their first meeting. She lowered her voice as if sharing a secret. "They jiggle."

"They what?"

"You heard me. Cold cuts jiggle. Except hard salami, but if I make an exception for that, the others will think I've caved."

"This is preposterous, you know."

"I've been told that before. And yet, it's true, so if you want me to come and hang out with you and those adorable, somewhat naughty children, no cold-cut platter, okay?"

"What about pizza?" he asked. "Do you have any qualms about pepperoni or mozzarella cheese?"

"Homemade?"

"My mother's recipe."

"I couldn't be more 'in' if I tried." She sounded downright excited about the idea of pizza and toddlers. He couldn't help himself.

He laughed. "Pizza it is. Sunday, after eleven."

"Yes, and I'll let you know what Christa says about the dress shopping then, okay?"

"Perfect." He hung up the phone, still grinning. For a minute, he thought she was going to be a salad kind of woman, and he didn't remember a day when Serenity wasn't on his case for his eating habits. He'd laughed then, because at six foot two and two hundred pounds, he liked food. And anyone who got that excited over pizza and kids was okay in his book.

Emily pulled into Grant's driveway at quarter past eleven on Sunday morning. She grabbed a cloth bag from the passenger seat, got out and surveyed her surroundings.

Nothing about this house said children lived there. A classic sprawling ranch with arched ceilings and south-facing skylights, impeccable landscaping and hand-laid paver walkways between gardens suggested the grass was not to be walked on. No toys lay scattered around the yard, and no tiny muddy shoes lined the elegant porch. The exterior of the house said appearances mattered, and that surprised her. She rang the bell and waited. And waited. And waited.

Was he here? Had he forgotten? Had something happened?

She was just about to ring the bell again, when the garage door started rolling up. "Emily?"

She moved down the steps and across the walk. "It's me." She entered a garage that didn't look nearly as HGTV pristine and saw Grant at the back door.

"Sorry, Timmy built a really cool tower by the front door and I'd have to ruin it or move it to open the door, and either one would probably launch a third world war. I figured we'd wait at least five minutes before we engaged in two-year-old histrionics. I'm glad you came."

He sounded delightfully normal and sincere, so she didn't tell him she'd weighed the invitation for the past twenty-four hours. She'd left the gray-stoned church still unsure, but she'd given her word and here she was. She stepped into a busy kitchen and instantly felt better. "This is more like it."

His brow knit, puzzled. "More like what?"

"The front of the house looks like a no-kid zone. This doesn't."

"Oh." He made a face as he shut the door. "The house and yard were from our upscale phase when Serenity was sure children weren't going to be part of the equation. It's not exactly a kid-friendly house or location, there's no one around to play with, but life's been too busy to think about moving. Although it's on the list," he finished.

Dolly was in the next room, systematically dumping bins of toys onto the floor, while Timmy was strategically placing large, locking plastic blocks on top of one another in a row of towers. "Here's your perfect example of the differences between these two, playing out right in front of you," Emily said softly.

He followed her gaze. "Two kids playing. Nothing too earth-shattering there, right?"

"Timmy is on the floor, focused and intent, creating structures, then placing them where he wants them. If he doesn't like the effect, he moves the little building and re-creates the scene."

"You're making block towers seem pretty sophisticated, Emily." He grinned and reached for her jacket, then hung it up. "And while every father wants their kid to be a rocket scientist or cure cancer, I think we've got a ways to go."

"Timmy's play is sophisticated for a young two-year-old. It shows memory, thought and process, then rearranging as needed, which means reasoning. Dolly's dumping is more along the lines of your typical one-year-old, seeing bright things, dumping bright things, then overwhelmed by the melee and unable to put the bright things away."

"She hates picking up and she loves destroying anything Tim makes. Which is what she's about to do right now." He crossed the room quickly, scooped Dolly up, told her no and set her back down.

She dropped to her knees instantly, turned and aimed for Tim's plastic block city.

Once again Grant intervened as Emily withdrew a set of finger cymbals from her bag. She stepped into the room, sat down on the floor and chinged the tiny instruments together.

Dolly turned, drawn to the sound. "Ba?"

"Music." Emily tapped the tiny cymbals together rapidly, happy, dancing notes floating through the air. "Music."

"Ba!" Dolly race-crawled her way as fast as she could go. "So ba!"

"You like music, Dolly-girl?" Emily raised her hand up, operating the metallic circles just out of Dolly's reach.

Dolly grabbed Emily's arm, intent on the noise. She pulled herself up to her knees, mesmerized by Emily's action. "Ba! Ba! Ba!"

"Music," Emily repeated and eased herself up onto the couch. "Ding! Ding! Ding! Music."

"Ting! Ting!" Dolly screeched the word, excited, then pulled herself up to a standing position, trying to get closer to the noise again. "Ting!"

Emily reached her free hand into her bag and brought out a little bell for Grant. "Ring this and move over there," she told him as she kept the flashy little cymbals playing. "Just far enough away so she might think about walking."

She didn't look at him to see if he was uncertain because even if he was, she wasn't. The thought of Dolly not achieving all God created her for was too sad to contemplate, so she wouldn't think about it. Grant wouldn't have requested her advice if he didn't recognize the problem, so that was a big first step.

She stopped making music when Grant was in position and pointed to him. He rang the bell, a lilting, joyful sound. Dolly turned, surprised to hear music from behind. "Ba! Ting!"

"Music," Grant told her, following Emily's lead. "Ding-dong, ding-dong, ding-dong!"

"Ting!" Dolly laughed and reached. "Ting!"

"Good talking," said Emily. "Go get the bell, Dolly. Go get it from Daddy."

"Ting." Dolly looked at her, then Grant and her forehead furrowed. "Ting! Ting! Ba!"

"You can have the bell if you go get it," Emily told her. Dolly was clinging to the couch with one hand, fully standing on her own. "Go get it, sweet thing."

"Ba!" Dolly's face darkened as she realized what they wanted. Emily had to hand it to the kid, for a two-year-old with developmental problems, Dolly could work the crowd. "Bee, ba. Beeeees."

"She's saying please," Grant told Emily. "She knows she's supposed to, but rarely does it. Should I give her the bell?"

"Did she walk to you?"

He frowned and when he did, it was Dolly's frown, just bigger and even more concerned.

"Toughen up, Dad."

"It's hard," he muttered, but he stood his ground. "Come get it, Doll-face."

"Oh, what a cute nickname. I love it."

Dolly wasn't impressed with their banter. She noticed her brother playing quietly and quickly dropped down. She took off in his direction.

Grant jangled the bell softly, intermittently. She whirled around, still on all fours, assessing the situation. At that moment, Emily understood part of Grant's problem. Because Dolly's appearance was more normal than most kids with her challenges, the expectation for her to process normally was high. Grant had mentioned that.

But the bright look in her eye indicated she

was doing a mental assessment, much like Emily had noticed at the office when they first met, and that could mean her reasoning was probably in the higher subnormal range. Either way, Dolly was sizing up the situation and making a choice, and that was pretty solid behavior to work with. She worked the cymbals again, then slid back to the floor. "Come here, precious."

"Ba!" Dolly crawled back her way, pulled herself up on Emily, patted her cheek and smiled. "Oh, ba!"

"You're pretty, too," Emily interpreted, smiling. "Here you go." She handed Dolly a pair of slightly bigger cymbals and showed her how to clang them. "Ding! Ding! Ding!"

To take the cymbals, Dolly had to let go of Emily and the couch. Emily put a shiny cymbal in each hand and when Grant called Dolly's name, she turned his way, beaming. "Ding! Ding!" She clapped the two cymbals together, off center, but close enough to create music. "Ding, Da!"

"You're making music, Doll-face." Grant smiled at her and he started to cross the room, but Emily shook her head.

"Stay right there. Squat down, open your arms and call her, as if she comes running to you every day."

He sent her a funny look, but did it, and then...
Oh, then!

Dolly clanged her cymbals, grinned in delight and took a step as if she'd been doing it forever. Then she stopped, made music again and took another step, a happy smile brightening her face. She repeated the action until she got to Grant's side. "Doll-face, you did it! You walked to Daddy!"

"Ting! Ting! Da!"

"You made music and walked to Daddy, Dolly." Emily crossed the room and hugged her, then smiled right into her china-doll eyes. "You did it! Big girl!"

"I have some?" Timmy noticed the instruments, stood up and came their way. "Music for Tim?"

"Absolutely." Emily reached into her bag and withdrew a xylophone and a little horn. She showed him both instruments and let him pick. He picked the horn, then marched around the room, tooting and strutting, the leader of the band.

Dolly got down on all fours and followed him, but she couldn't keep up. Finally she sat back on her bottom and wailed.

"And this is where you would normally pick her up and move her closer, but let's see what she does if we just walk away," Emily whispered. She was close enough to Grant to note the way his hair curled around the back of his ear, enough to say Dolly's curls came from her daddy. When he followed her toward the kitchen, a whiff of some inviting, guy-scented soap took precedence over old breakfast dishes.

Dolly fussed and scolded in unintelligible gibberish, while Tim kept marching. She looked at them.

They pretended not to notice.

"Da!" she yelled, but without her normal force.

They ignored her, talking quietly.

She stared across the room where Emily had left her cymbals at the edge of the couch, an invitation to join the band if ever there was one. She crawled over, head down, determined, and when she got to the couch, she pulled herself up and grabbed the cymbals.

Emily reached for Grant's hand. "I think she's going to do it."

"You think?" Grant whispered the words close to her cheek, close enough to feather her hair with coffee-scented breath. "How—?"

He stopped talking as Dolly clapped her cymbals together twice in a row, and then took a tiny step forward. "Ding!" She yelled the word, paused, banged her cymbals and took another tiny step. "Ding! Ding!"

Timmy didn't notice. He was too busy marching and tooting.

"Ding!" She yelled it again, but as she took another step forward, she almost giggled. "Ding!" Step. "Ding!" Step. "Ding! Ding!" Step. Step. Step.

And now Timmy noticed. His hazel eyes went wide and he tooted his horn and pointed. "Dowwy, good! Dowwy, good! Yay!"

Grant stayed silent and still behind Emily, and for a few seconds she thought he was upset or angry. Then she turned.

Damp-eyed, he watched his little girl as she tried to follow her more adept brother around the room. She couldn't keep up, but it didn't matter. Tim marched around the outer perimeter, leading his imaginary band. Dolly made a much smaller circle in the middle, but she was walking, all by herself, and playing with her brother.

"How'd you know what to do?" Grant whispered. His gruff voice sounded emotional and not a little chagrined. "Has she been fooling me like her occupational therapist has suggested?"

"Therapist-1, Grant-0," Emily replied, just as soft. "Her good looks inspire people to take care of her. But of course, in the end, that doesn't do her any good because you want her to be as independent as she possibly can be. To shoot for the stars."

"And have her chronically disappointed?"

Emily snorted, then laughed at his expression. "Listen, Mr. Glass-Half-Empty, struggle builds character and character builds strength. With her problems, she's going to need to be as strong as possible. Your job is to see she gets that way, even if you have to wipe a few tears."

"I hate seeing her cry," he told her.

"I meant your tears," she teased, laughing, and jabbed his arm gently. "Letting go is tough. But necessary. Absolutely, positively necessary."

Chapter Six

~

Others had said similar things. Several times, in fact. Why did he finally listen when it came from Emily? What was it about her that made sense? She might not be an expert, but somehow, her opinion mattered. He wasn't sure why, but he'd promised her lunch and it was almost twelve thirty. "We should do lunch, shouldn't we?"

"What time are their naps?"

"In about an hour."

She nodded. "Then yes, and if you won't be insulted, you can make food while I load the dishwasher. Four hands go faster than two, and it's anybody's guess how long we have." Her quick glance into the front room indicated the toddlers.

"True enough. And pizza's okay?"

"Way better than okay. Especially if it's homemade."

"One of my few culinary talents. That and red sauce. I should have been born Italian, but Irish and German won the day."

"I'm a Gallagher, so Irish works for me, Grant." She filled the top rack with sippy cups and coffee mugs and tiny bowls. "I've chatted with Christa over the computer, and next Tuesday morning at ten seems like the best time."

"I can't deny being a little intimidated by the thought of going to a bridal store—"

"Salon."

"Bridal salon," he corrected himself in a long, dry tone, "and shopping for a dress. Awkward."

"It won't be awkward at all—it will be nice. Caroline's excited that Christa's getting married and can't wait to pull dresses that might work. And she's hooking up the computer to a bigger screen so we'll actually be able to see Christa if all goes well."

"This is only one of the many times I wish my mother was here." Grant layered sauce and cheese on the rolled dough. "She should be here to do this stuff, to see her daughter get married. My father left because he wanted to. Mom didn't have a choice."

"Family stuff gets hard, doesn't it?" Emily bent to fill the lower dishwasher tray. "I used to be so jealous of my big brother. Dave was good at everything he did. Sports, music, school. And then he was gone and I couldn't get over the guilt of being jealous for a long time. Forgiving someone who hurts you or the ones you love is tough. And the more important they are, the harder it is to forgive and forget."

"No sense worrying about forgiving someone who abandons you, is there?" Grant shrugged. "My father made a choice and stuck by it. I can't imagine wanting anything to do with him. He had his chance to be part of the family. He blew it. End of story."

Ouch.

Emily took a mental step back.

Wasn't forgiveness part of life? Part of being a good person?

Can you honestly say you've forgiven Christopher for dumping you and having his father dismiss you from your job?

A part of her knew he'd done her a favor, but she hadn't felt that way eighteen months ago. Time and prayer had helped heal her.

But Grant was talking a three-decades-old hurt. Harboring a grudge that long couldn't be healthy, but what did she know? Her parents had been together nearly forty years. Hers was only the second divorce in their family in two decades, and that wasn't a sought-after distinction.

Besides, she wasn't privy to the details. In that case, erring on the side of caution was best, but his rigid attitude concerned her. Forgiveness was a part of life, and a huge part of reconciliation. Relationships without forgiveness were doomed before they started.

You're not looking for a relationship, remember? You're looking for respect, recognition and appreciation for a job well-done.

Her goal wasn't easy when her older sister was a paragon in the event industry, while Emily was more like a fledgling. But she was learning. "Done." She finished loading the dishes and wiped the counter as Grant spread more cheese over the sauce-covered fresh dough. "That smells wonderful and it hasn't even started baking yet."

"It's this." He held out the bowl of fresh mozzarella and Parmesan. "This blend is perfect, and I get it hand done at Luigi's."

"Best Italian food on the lake," she declared. "Their ravioli alone are enough to die for."

"Not much romance in killing your date," he supposed with a wink as he slid the tray into the top side of the double oven. "But the food is great. Or was," he corrected himself. "Our food tasting last week was the first night I've been out to eat since these guys were born."

"Over two years?"

He winced a little. "Put that way, it sounds awful, doesn't it?" He shrugged. "But life's busy and I'd rather spend my time with the kids. But of course—" and this time he aimed a very direct gaze her way "—those things take on a different spin if you're in very special company."

She pretended to misread his meaning intentionally. "Good company is never a bad thing."

"A bestseller on a rainy night is good company." He leaned over and smiled at her, unafraid to make his point. "*Very special company* is different. That's when you have the chance to talk to a pretty girl and you actually sit down and do it."

"I don't expect that happens all that often, either, though," she said as he went back to arranging pepperoni while Dolly attempted to wrestle the horn from her brother. "Unless the pretty girl stops by the highway department now and again."

"Or your house, to talk about kids." He didn't look up from arranging the pepperoni in even, concentric circles, but his grin underscored his meaning.

Heat crept up her cheeks, but when Dolly put a wrestling move on Tim, Emily didn't have time to worry about flirtations or really nice-looking overprotective fathers because she had to move quick to save Timmy from his sister's wrath.

And by the time Grant had calmed Timmy down and put Dolly in her high chair munching on a peanut-butter-and-jelly sandwich, she figured she'd read too much into his words.

"Em, can you check that pizza?"

She opened the oven and peeked in. "Almost, but not quite. Shall I set the timer again? Give it another few minutes?"

"That would be great." He handed sippy cups to both kids. "So what do you think about this one?" He slanted a quiet gaze down to Dolly. "Will she just walk automatically now?"

"She'll probably need encouragement every step of the way until she breaks the habit of begging to be carried. Just say no."

He winced. "Possible fail expected."

She waggled her finger at him. "Be tough. Don't think about today—focus on tomorrow. That's important with kids, but especially with kids who have developmental issues."

"If you know so much about this and love kids, why go into business?" he wondered, and he didn't seem interrogatory. Just—curious.

"By the time I realized I was good at this and liked it, I was three years into my degree. So I stayed the course. And I like buying and looking forward to what folks will love, want or need eighteen months in advance. I enjoy having a window on the fashion world, my own sneak preview. Wipe that expression right off your face—there is nothing wrong with liking nice clothes, or finding nice clothes that look good on women of all sizes for an affordable price. You've got it in your head that it's all about me."

He frowned as if ready to argue, and she raised a hand for quiet.

"I have been fighting the pageant-princess image for years. I might have to do it forever, who knows? If I'd been skilled at soccer or the violin or debate, people wouldn't look at me and see an empty head on a good body."

His smile said he appreciated the good body, and she couldn't help but laugh then she sobered. "The thing is, the skill set to nail pageant wins is partially earned and partially due to God-given attributes. But isn't that true for everything we do? The big, burly linebacker owes part of his success to body type. The amazing cellist might owe part of her talent to her parents' genetics. In my case, I like being on stage, I'm good with people, I can dance and I think fast on my feet. Turning all of that into a free ride at NYU was a smart thing to do."

* * *

It was, he admitted to himself, but he hesitated to agree because of his experience with Serenity. As a broadcaster, a good appearance was part of the job. She'd taken it to extremes, making good looks the baseline for everything. Him, her, the house, the yard. There was no arguing with her, so he went along with it most of the time. She took offense easily and would spend days in a silent, pouting mode. A change of subject would be best, he decided. "Your stint at the children's center opened my eyes, Emily. With more than the great smile and really nice jeans," he added.

"Good jeans are important in any closet." She laughed. She glanced at the clock and frowned. "I've got to head out. I've got some things to take care of for Kimberly's wedding, and I promised I'd get them done this afternoon. Can I take my pizza to go?"

"You have to go? Really? Or did we just scare you completely away when Dolly started painting her high chair with grape jelly?"

Emily took a soft, warm washcloth from his hands and wiped Dolly down. "I don't scare easy, Grant."

"Is that the truth?" He bent around her at the sink, to see her face. "Because it's not just one big old scarred and kind of rusty heart in this house."

She met his gaze, counted the tiny flecks of green and yellow softening the deep gray around his pupil, and swallowed a sigh because Emily Gallagher didn't sigh. Ever.

"It's three," he continued softly. "And that makes a big difference."

"It does," she answered quietly. "And you and I have rocked the romance boat in the past with little success."

"These guys were my amazingly wonderful, tiny lifeboats."

She smiled in the twins' directions. "Reason enough to stay afloat, right here. But we've both been burned, Grant. And we're both cautious. Maybe too cautious, but that's how it is." She slipped out from beneath his arm and retrieved her jacket.

"Does this mean no Italian food dinner date?" he asked as he set two slices of pizza onto a paper plate. "Because one of us was serious about that, Em."

The steady look he gave her made her heart go unsteady. There was strength in this man. Commitment was his mainstay; he was rock solid.

But he didn't go to church, he couldn't forgive his father and he was feet-in-concrete stubborn.

She accepted the pizza, but not the date. "A discussion we can pursue at a later time. I'm going to leave the bag of musical instruments here for Tim and Dolly to play with, okay? I borrowed them from Rory's summertime pre-K stuff, so I have to give them back, but she won't need them until she does next year's session. If you don't mind the noise."

He grinned in the kids' direction. "Noise concerns went out the window when these two came in the door."

She liked that. His sacrificial nature with kids was a real blessing. Kids should always come first, shouldn't they?

Her phone suddenly beeped with a text alert. She glanced at it and frowned. "Wedding stuff. Gotta go. We're six days out from Kimberly and Drew's wedding, and who'd have thought the wedding planner would get the jitters? But she has and I'm needed." She accepted the plate of pizza, smooched both kids on their sticky cheeks and headed to the door. "So next Tuesday, ten a.m. unless you hear differently, okay?"

"I'll be there."

"Good. And don't forget the wedding invite for next Saturday, okay? A family invite." She jerked a thumb toward the twins and left before the temptation to have a Sunday afternoon with Grant and those two kids proved too strong to resist.

She recognized her attraction to Grant. And she saw it was two-sided. But two people with issues of trust and forgiveness needed to heed the warning signs God posted along the side of the romance road.

He wanted to take her out on a date. She wanted to go.

How she wished it could be that easy.

"When are Mom and Dad getting in for the wedding?" Emily asked as she tied an extravagant number of tiny ribbons into minute bows later that afternoon. "I know they had to change their flight to accommodate the doctor's appointment in Houston."

"Eleven fifteen on Tuesday at the Rochester airport. Can you pick them up?" Kimberly narrowed her mouth as her attempt at ribbon tying ended in failure. She growled as she tossed the wrinkled ribbon across the room.

"I can't. I'm meeting with Stella Yorkos about her wedding shower, and I can't even imagine how you're handling her wedding because she's three shades of crazy over a fairly simple event."

"Give her anything she wants to keep her reasonably happy." When Emily winced, Kimberly sighed. "There's really no other way around the Stellas of this world, Em. Trust me on this."

"It doesn't bother you, how she argues about everything? The prices, the look, the presentation? Nothing is ever right."

"Welcome to my world," said Kimberly, which was exactly why Emily didn't fit in. She didn't like arguing or bartering. She liked peace and contentment. Making people happy.

"I'll pick up Mom and Dad." Their widowed sister-in-law Corinne raised a hand as she made a list the old-fashioned way with paper and a pen. "The kids are in school and we'll be back here in time to help with whatever Kimberly's fussing over at that particular moment."

"I don't fuss."

Emily, Corinne and Rory exchanged looks and kept their mouths shut.

Kimberly opened a box, stared at the contents and promptly burst into tears. She grabbed a handful of tissues and wiped her face. "But these are the most hideous little boxes for wedding favors I've ever seen. What was I thinking?"

Emily let Rory put an arm of comfort around the oldest Gallagher, while she and Corinne looked inside the box.

"Did you order these on purpose? Because if you did, I'm having your vision checked."

"That's not what they looked like on the website."

Corinne brought up the website that promised high-quality boxware, perfect for country chic weddings. "They lied."

"You think?" Kimberly dabbed her eyes and blew her nose. "I can't believe this—the wedding is six days away, and I don't care that it's not big and fancy, but I wanted it at least somewhat tasteful. And homey. And mine."

She teared up again. Emily slipped an arm around her and sat her down. "I am officially taking over the final details of your wedding. You will hate me now but thank me later. For this week, you will be the treasured bride, the numero uno of customers, preparing for your special, special day."

The use of their wry wedding term made Kimberly smile through her tears.

"These will be shipped back, and your job this week is to focus on the Schreiner wedding in December, map out details, etc. That way you're busy and not thinking of how totally hot Drew Slade will look in his tux."

"He's gorgeous, isn't he?"

"Beyond that," Corinne agreed, smiling.

"And the kid's a total bonus," added Rory.

"Listen, about favors. A lot of brides are doing simple favors, then listing a spot where they made a donation to a charity. That's a really nice way of giving folks a memento without breaking the bank and helping others at the same time. If you want to do that, I can design a graphic for you to put on the table."

"Jelly jars," Corinne suggested. "We could get those cute little jars of jam and jelly, then tag them with the charity's name and logo."

"Can we do that this close to the wedding?" Kimberly asked, then went silent when Emily nailed her with a fierce look.

"Can and will. I'm in charge now. Remember?"

Kimberly nodded, almost meek, and Emily couldn't remember a time when her big sister was ever meek. "Mags needs to be brushed. Consider it therapy. We'll plan this out and you'll love it. I promise. Micromanaging every little thing just because you're a crazy-efficient event planner is only going to make you insane."

"You're right." Kimberly stood, dropped her pencil and picked up the little Yorkie. "If you guys don't mind, I'll go over to the carriage house and watch football with my beloved. And his cute kid. And the dogs."

"Best idea I've heard in a while." Emily hugged her, and hugging her sister felt a whole lot better than their past squabbles. "You focus on Drew and writing your vows. We'll finish up these last-minute details."

"Okay."

Corinne waited until Kimberly had crossed the yard and disappeared into the carriage house before she burst out laughing. "Who'd have thought?"

"I know," agreed Emily. "The great and mighty Wizard of Oz has fallen. The best part is that we'll be able to hold this over her head for years." Emily grinned as she pulled up a page featuring jams, then paused. "Wait. One of the Mennonite women has been doing this kind of thing for Brian's farm store on East Lake Road. Gabby mentioned it to me." Their cousin Brian Gallagher had developed a thriving farm market on the southeast end of the lake. His converted barn housed goods and wares from the entire agricultural and craft community.

"Yes." Rory nodded as she retaped the carton of wretched-looking miniature boxes. "They donate gift boxes to lots of charity events."

"Rory, can you see if they can fill the order for a hundred-and-forty four-ounce jars of assorted jams and jellies with gold lids by Friday? That way we're keeping business local. The cookies that were going to go into the boxes can be put out on trays, and we'll have Kimberly and Drew pick a charity." She texted her sister, not really expecting a quick response, but when Kimberly's reply came through, Emily smiled. "They want the donation to be made to the 9/11 Memorial to honor fallen first responders."

Corinne paused. So did Rory. They looked at each other, then away. Corinne broke the silence. "You'd think after more than ten years, it wouldn't get to me, wouldn't you? You'd think I'd be able to just shrug the whole thing off now. Losing Dave, having him gone. But every now and again it hits like a wall of bricks, falling on my head."

"You don't date, Corinne." Emily didn't want to pry, but they'd lost her brother and Corinne's husband in a drug sting gone bad over a decade ago. "Ever. Why?"

"Who's got time?" She sat down and splayed her hands. "I loved your brother—he was larger-than-life, and so much fun, but it's not like I'm putting him on a pedestal or something. I've got two kids and a hospital job working nights so I can be with them as much as possible. Time flies by and they're more important than anything. I kind of go along for the ride. And besides, what if I picked the wrong person? Not for me. For them. Is anything really worth that risk?"

Grant had said a similar thing, and Emily had

never really thought about it from a single parent's point of view. "Is it a trust in God thing? Or fear of making a mistake?"

"Both, I guess, but that's a valid fear," Corinne told them. "The heart's a fickle organ. I'm a trauma nurse. I know these things."

They shared a smile.

"You must get lonely sometimes, don't you?" Emily asked.

Corinne swiped a hand to her eyes, then shrugged. "Everybody gets lonely. My time will come—I believe that. More than anything, I want my children's futures secured. Tee and Callan are God's gift to me, and I want to do whatever's in my power to help them succeed. Which reminds me, the Smiths are dropping Callan off here in a little while. And Tee needs a ride home from Cassidy's house in an hour." She set her phone alarm. "For the moment, let's talk nothing but weddings, smiles and joy. Dad's cancer gave us a real heads-up. We don't do any of this on our time…so let's make the best use of the time we've got."

"True," said Rory. "Brian's website says their shop is open until five, so I'm going to take a quick ride out there and check things out, okay? Then I'll work on the graphic when I get back. If all goes well, we should have them ordered and the labels ready before the night's over."

"Without drama," noted Emily.

Rory made a face of disbelief. "Weddings and drama go hand in hand. One of the many reasons I'm not a fan of the industry. Crazy begets crazy. Give me a simpler world, every time."

Corinne didn't disagree. "Four women, one wedding. Oh, Em, darling…drama just goes with the territory."

Grant called her Em, too.

And he said it in a tone like they were close friends. Or sweethearts.

Her phone buzzed with a text. It was Grant, sending her a picture of the twins, playing side by side, both standing.

She laughed, and Corinne peeked over her shoulder. "Oh, they're adorable! Are those Grant McCarthy's kids?"

"Yes."

"Oh, I could just smooch them to pieces," Rory exclaimed as she grabbed up her purse to go. "What a pair of sweethearts."

"They are," she agreed. "Beyond special. And different as night and day."

"Oh, really?" Corinne exchanged amused looks with Rory, and Emily raised a hand to stave off their speculation.

"All kids are delightful."

"Grant's kind of cute himself," Corinne noted. "Of course, you probably haven't noticed that."

"I can't stop noticing that," Emily mumbled. "Which is ridiculous. Right?"

"Or amazingly perfect in God's eyes," Rory told her. "I'm leaving, and we put the lid on drama, remember?"

"This isn't drama, this is romance," Corinne said. "You go. I'll live vicariously through Emily's romance with Grant."

"There is no romance," Emily insisted. And even if she wanted there to be, it couldn't happen. It was tough enough to prove herself in the world of wedding planning. None of it came naturally to her. And Kate & Company would be her sister's gig, once life settled down.

It was easy to love the town of Grace Haven. Not just because she'd grown up here, but because it was a great place to live.

You need a job. You loved your work at Barrister's. Don't sell yourself short.

She was in danger of doing exactly that, like a young bird coming back to the nest.

She couldn't let comfort dictate her choices. Hadn't she just told Grant the same thing about Dolly? She'd have to chart her own course and try not to mess up too much in the meantime.

Chapter Seven

A steady snowfall blanketed the town in the wee hours before Kimberly's wedding. Pure and pristine, the gentle coating whitewashed every outdoor nook and cranny. Cold, but not too cold, and not a breath of wind stirred the snow outlining tree branches, fencing and rooflines. In the space of a few hours, Grace Haven had become a winter paradise and a photographer's dream.

Drew's eleven-year-old daughter, Amy, began the happy church procession, followed by Rory and Emily. Their mother, Kate, smiled from her front-row pew, dabbed tears, then smiled again. When Kimberly appeared in the doorway, she smiled up at her dad, then shifted that smile to her beloved groom. The guests uttered a collective sigh.

This was you, nearly four years ago. What happened?

Emily had no answers, only more questions. As Kimberly took her place beside Drew, her love and longing mirrored his. They exchanged a look of sweet devotion.

Emily's heart pinched tight, even as she smiled, glad for her sister's happiness.

She'd wanted that, maybe too much. The lure of being a rich man's wife, the mistress of a beautiful country estate… She'd been wooed as much by prestige as romance. And the fact that she'd one-upped her sister had ranked high on her radar back then. The realization embarrassed her.

When she followed the wedding party back down the aisle, Kimberly hugged her right off. "Thank you. You made this all come together and kept me from being a total wreck. I love you, Emily."

She couldn't remember the last time her sister had used those words. She hugged her back and repeated the phrase. "I love you, too. And you are an absolutely wonderful, beautiful, radiant bride."

Tears glistened in Kimberly's eyes. "Knock it off," Emily ordered. "If you ruin that mascara, I'll—" Emily couldn't possibly think of an appropriate threat so she smiled, instead. "I'll fix it, of course."

They did a quick winter-scene photography session before they arrived at the reception site, and who was waiting there when the limousine dropped off the small wedding party?

Grant, with Timmy and Dolly.

"You came!" She shouldn't be this excited to see them, but she was. She hurried across the foyer, then bent and hugged each of the kids. "I can't believe you braved it, Grant."

"Tillie helped." He looked downright nervous as people began streaming in. "If they get too crazy, I can take them home, Em."

"With over a hundred adults here, I expect we can keep them amused."

"Grant." Kate Gallagher crossed the room and grasped his hands. "I'm so glad you could come and delighted to have these two with us! Pete, do you see who's here?"

Emily's dad crossed the floor more slowly than he used to. "Grant. You clean up nice."

"As do you, sir."

"Which table are you at? I'd enjoy having you at ours."

"He's at mine, Dad." Emily ruffled Tim's hair as she straightened.

Her father turned, and the look he leveled on

her, then Grant, assessed the situation. "I see. And I heard that our little Dolly is walking. Is this true?" He bent low to look into Dolly's sweet face.

She squeezed against her father's leg, but smiled at him.

"Thanks to Emily." Grant's tone expressed the depth of his gratitude. "I was playing the part of the overprotective father and she called me on it." The look he gave her, as if she'd done something wonderful, made her want to do more wonderful things. "Before you knew it, Dolly was walking."

"I tricked her into it." Emily winked at her dad. "I took a page out of your playbook, Dad."

Pete put an arm around her shoulders in a hug that wasn't as strong as it used to be. Everything she'd read said this was normal with his course of treatment. Emily prayed the information was correct. "That's my girl."

Dolly moved from Grant's pant leg to Emily's gown. "Bees?" She lifted her arms to Emily, asking to be picked up.

Grant reached down to extricate her. "Em's all dressed up. We don't want to get stuff on her dress, Doll-face."

Emily lifted the little girl and held her close. "I'm pretty sure this dress will never be hauled out of the closet again, the majority of pictures are done and I've got a few moments of freedom. Considering all that, Dolly and I are going to have this dance." She swooped and turned with the toddler, dipping her, moving in time with the music.

Dolly laughed. She laughed loud and long, clapping her hands, delighted with her new friend.

And Emily felt the same way about her and Timmy.

Beautiful together.

Emily in her long black gown and Dolly in her pink smocked dress.

Mixed emotions rocked Grant. Emily seemed so comfortable with the little girl. So natural.

That should make him happy, and it did, but the thought of Serenity making the opposite choice still burned. He'd married a beautiful woman who turned her back on them because she didn't want to deal with motherhood and Dolly's limitations.

Anger gnawed at him. He should be a bigger man. Shove it aside, cast it away.

He couldn't. Having his ex-wife walk away from her family didn't just break his heart. It made him mad, because they were given an amazing opportunity to love two children.

And she still walked away.

Tim grabbed his pant leg and pulled him forward as the DJ put on a faster song. "Timmy dance!"

Tim rocked it with Grant. He laughed, marching and dancing with awkward feet, having the time of his life. And when the music slowed for the next song, Corinne took Timmy and Rory scooped up Dolly.

Which left him and Emily, three feet apart and no toddlers to distract them. He opened his arms and took a step forward. "May I have this dance, Em?"

She breathed deep, holding his gaze, and for a moment he thought she might say no, but then she stepped into his arms and put her hand in his.

Spiced vanilla with a hint of berry. She smelled absolutely wonderful, and to have her in his arms, moving gently to the music, made him think it would be wonderful to have her in his arms all the time. It felt right. It felt good. Holding her, moving with her, touched his heart in a way he'd forgotten, long ago. She made the children laugh, made them learn and made him want to be a better man, a better person.

She's leaving, remember? She made that clear.

But what if she had reason to stay, he wondered. What if being with him and the twins was enough of a reason to stay?

He didn't want the song to end, but it did, and Emily was called away to do maid of honor chores. By the time the twins had eaten a few bites of dinner, it was time for Grant to take them home.

He caught up to Emily as Kimberly and Drew were cutting the cake. "We're approaching meltdown time," he whispered. Her quick smile said she understood. "Instinct tells me that's better handled in a controlled environment."

She laughed and grabbed her cape from the coat rack. "I'll help you get them in the car."

"No, Em. It's cold. It's—"

"Thank you, Em. That's very nice of you." She held his attention until he caved.

"I do thank you. And it is nice of you."

"I know." She shot him a smile over her shoulder. When the cold outside air hit them, she bundled Timmy against her shoulder and hurried to the car.

"Your shoes are going to be wet."

"Not the first time that's happened. Won't be the last." She tucked Timmy into his car seat and buckled the harness into place while Grant did the same thing for Dolly. "It was a beautiful wedding," she noted as she swept Timmy's cheek with butterfly kisses. He laughed up at her, clearly delighted. So was Grant. "Everything came off without a hitch. I'm happy and tired."

"You did great."

She shrugged off the compliment. "Kimberly's plans—I just implemented them. But it went well, and that's what counts."

"Will I see you before the appointment at the bridal salon?"

She shook her head. "Mom and Dad are only here until Monday. Dad's due back in Houston for the next treatment, and they won't be coming back for the holidays. I want to spend as much time with them as I can."

"Then I'll see you Tuesday. Thanks for spending time with us, Em."

She looked up as he rounded the car.

Those eyes, bright and brown, full of life. Her hair, a tumble of auburn, half tamed by the hairdresser, half wild and free. Snowflakes sifted gently, here and there, dusting her shoulders, her hair.

She met his gaze, and for the life of him he couldn't look away. He didn't want to look away.

"Emily? They're going to throw the bouquet!" Two young Gallagher cousins hung out the door of the inn, waving to get her attention.

He smiled and lifted his hand to graze her cheek lightly. "Next time." He dropped his gaze to her lips, then sighed, smiling.

"You think so?" She grinned up at him, teasing, and right then Grant was pretty sure he could enjoy a lifetime of that teasing.

"Let's just say..." He cradled her cool cheek with one big hand and held her gaze. "I hope so, Em. I dearly hope so."

Her eyes went wide. She swallowed hard.

So did he.

She turned and hurried inside, but when she got to the top step, she turned and waved.

Seeing her framed in the doorway of the rustic country inn was one of the prettiest sights he'd ever seen. Her long black gown, fitted just so, the glorious auburn hair, the dark green cloak, the clutch of flowers in her hair.

Breathtaking.

He had no trouble understanding the pageant wins, not at this moment, because Grant McCarthy was 100 percent sure he'd never seen a more beautiful woman in his life. What worried him most was that he saw that as more of a negative than a positive.

What kind of man thought like that?

The kind that had watched beauty slam the door on him before.

Three small suitcases lined the back entry when Emily came downstairs Monday morning. "You're all set, then?" She reached out and hugged her mother, then her father.

"Yes, and Corinne's pulling in right now. What a wonderful time we had, being home." Her mother hugged her again, then Rory. "You girls did an amazing job on that wedding. Your father and I were so impressed."

"And Kimberly didn't go ballistic, so we count that as a win," Rory teased. She hugged their dad, then pseudo scolded him. "You focus on getting well. We've got this all under control here."

"I see that. I'm actually feeling a little useless." He smiled and hugged each of them in turn. "You guys are doing a great job, and that's a big relief. Heaven only knows what I'd be doing if my wife was worrying over her business."

Kate scolded him with a look.

Pete laughed and shrugged an arm around her. "You girls are keeping your mother sane, and that's the best get-well gift a man could want. We'll keep you posted, but so far, so good, and that's the answer we're looking for."

They left, talking, then laughing together, as if facing life and death wasn't taking a toll.

"That's the kind of faith-filled marriage I'd love to have someday." Rory spoke softly, watching them go to the car.

Realization hit Emily.

Her parents' marriage wasn't strong because

they'd both had good jobs, great careers and lived in a sweet, small town. It was strong because they put God first, always. They believed and then tried to live their beliefs every single day.

The Barristers weren't churchgoing people. She'd shrugged that off as nonessential when she'd accepted Christopher's proposal—a foolish mistake. Seeing her parents cleared up that *glass darkly* the Bible talked about. Faith wasn't something a married couple conveniently grabbed off the shelf as needed.

Faith was lived.

An image of Grant and those two kids came to mind. He didn't take them to church, nor did he go himself. He didn't profess faith or belief.

He'd mocked himself for his past "upscale" life, a mistake she'd made, too. She'd been shallow and put prestige first. Had they both learned their lesson?

Maybe. But the faith question didn't just niggle her, it grabbed hold. She'd messed up once, and she didn't want to repeat her mistake. She liked Grant a lot. This wasn't a schoolgirl crush. When she was with Grant and those kids, it was all-out attraction, seeing a future laid out before them.

But she needed to take the rose-colored glasses off and toss them away because she'd been blinded by attraction before. Now she needed something deeper, something rooted in faith, hope and love. She was pretty sure Grant McCarthy wasn't ready to give that.

Dolly was walking everywhere.

Grant couldn't believe the difference ten days made. Greater mobility changed her attitude, making her a happier child. Mrs. Flanagan, the occupational therapist and Emily had all told him to push her forward. He hadn't, and he'd stunted her potential. Watching how quickly her motor skills progressed was inspiring. But now that she was more mobile, danger lurked everywhere.

Climbing. Getting down after climbing. Exploring. Wandering off. Her world got bigger and his job got harder, but the joy on her sweet face made it all worthwhile.

He needed to thank Emily for that final push. He could bring flowers to Caroline's bridal shop, but what if he embarrassed her? She'd had a crazy week with her sister's wedding. He wanted to be sensitive to that, and being sensitive was probably a habit he should develop.

He called Chloe's Floral Designs on Monday and ordered flowers delivered instead, with a picture of Dolly half walking, half running across their backyard in the first light snow.

Arms out, joy radiated from his beautiful child, despite her limitations. And who could say what Dolly might be able to achieve? No one knew for sure, so he needed to get on the bandwagon to cheer her on. If only his foolish heart didn't clench with every stumble, every fall.

"You made a difference, not just now…" he wrote on the card "…but for a long time to come. Look what you started! In deepest appreciation, Grant."

He tucked the photo into the card and handed it to Chloe to be delivered with the bouquet. He used to send flowers to his mother several times a year. Thanking her made him feel good. She'd put her kids first, and Grant had appreciated that.

He missed her, still. Planning Christa's wedding wasn't just a gift for Christa, it was a salute to one of the strongest women he'd ever known, Dolores McCarthy. He got back to the office Monday afternoon just in time to answer the phone. "Grace Haven Highway, Grant speaking."

"You never answer your own phone." Emily's voice greeted him, light and friendly. He sank into his chair, instantly more relaxed.

"I would if I knew it was you calling."

"Aww." He'd surprised her. *Good.* "I just got the flowers, Grant. Thank you."

"You're welcome. Do you see that picture? How happy my little girl looks? She's almost running now, Emily, and it hasn't been all that long. Dolly McCarthy, unleashed! It's amazing to see, and I wanted you to know how much it meant to me."

"I'm so glad. And yes, the look on her face is priceless. Are you geared up for wedding gown shopping tomorrow?"

"With you? Yes." She started to sputter, so he changed the subject. "Kimberly's reception was really nice. Thank you again for including us. I can't deny I was concerned about bringing the twin terrors to a formal affair."

"They were wonderful. I'm glad you braved it. Mom and Dad were pleased, too."

"Well, you did a great job, not just on that, but on everything. With your mom gone, you girls have really taken charge."

"Kimberly, mostly."

Grant disagreed quickly. "Kimberly isn't doing this alone. I saw the event calendar on your notebook, remember? To handle everything your mom had on the books, and the extras you girls pulled in, is kind of amazing, don't you think?"

"Well, I figured God put us in the right place at the right time. Who'd have thought Kimberly and Drew would be married now? Six months ago, it wasn't a blip on the radar, and now they're off on their honeymoon, which means I get to run the business and spoil their daughter, Amy, for a week."

Grant laughed. "You're good with kids. I hadn't expected that."

"I know what you expected." Emily's voice went light but dry. "Total airhead, self-absorbed princess."

"I was wrong. Beyond wrong. Possibly more wrong than any man should have the right to be. Forgive me?"

"Apology accepted. All is forgiven. Gotta go, much to do here without Kimberly. I'll see you tomorrow at ten."

He'd be there, all right. Excited to see her, because she made him smile, made him laugh and wasn't afraid to call him on things. She made him want to be a better person, and that didn't just feel good. It felt wonderful.

Chapter Eight

"You've ruined everything." Stella Yorkos stormed into Kate & Company just before four that afternoon, looking more like a bridezilla than any woman should. "I distinctly said I wanted three entrées for the shower, and look what you've sent out!" She waved the invitation toward Allison, then Emily.

Emily took the elaborate shower invite and the response card and frowned. "I'm not sure I understand the problem, Stella. There *are* three choices here, that you personally selected. 'Salmon with maple-glazed pecan quinoa,' 'Filet of beef with mushroom reduction' and 'Chicken Marsala.'"

"It's not what's there," Stella hissed and stabbed a finger toward the reply card. "There is no vegetarian entrée, and what kind of woman these days doesn't have a slew of friends who find eating anything with a face repugnant?"

Emily took a moment to breathe as she sorted this through. "Stella, you chose the dishes yourself. You approved the menu."

"I assumed a vegan or vegetarian option was a given! How am I supposed to know these things? I'm a lawyer, not some stupid party planner who doesn't know enough to explain things thoroughly. And now it's spoiled, all spoiled because people will think I'm not smart enough to have recognized their needs at my shower!"

A swift-moving headache started somewhere around Emily's toes and raced upward. "This is fixable, Stella. I'll call Roselawn and arrange for them to have a vegetarian option available. They make an excellent eggplant Parmesan casserole, and a marvelous mushroom and potato stew. I'd be glad to find out other possibilities for you."

"You don't get it." Stella slapped her hand against the top of Allison's desk and took a step closer. "It doesn't matter that they have it and can provide it. What matters are the appearances of the situation, as if I wasn't savvy enough to anticipate what others want. My mother is fit to be tied, my aunt is thrilled that I've messed up because that makes her daughter's wedding shower nicer by comparison and why a party-planning place can't get a simple function right is beyond me. I am so tempted." She pushed her face closer to Emily and scowled. "So very tempted to cancel everything and start over somewhere else. And don't spew your contract spiel with me. I'm a lawyer—I can wriggle out of that document in a heartbeat." She snapped her fingers for emphasis. "You tell me here, right now, what you're going to do to make this right, or I'm walking out that door, and my shower and my wedding go with me." She folded her arms tight across her chest and glowered, her right toe tapping an ominous beat against the tile floor.

What Emily wanted to do and what she could do were two very different things. She'd like to hand Stella the contract, wish her well and escort her out the door, but her father's pricey treatments in Houston might be the difference between life and death, and medical bills had to be paid.

Give her anything she wants.

Kimberly's words from the week before.

Emily looked at Allison. Allison lifted her shoulders, equally at odds. She turned back to Stella and lifted the response card. "First, I will resend the invitations at our expense."

"And?"

"And Kate & Company will be glad to cover the cost of the additional entrée with Roselawn."

"And?"

Nope, that was where Emily intended to draw the line. The large shower would cost a pretty penny this way, and they'd be kissing goodbye a good share of their profit. "And that's my offer."

"That's it?"

Emily had been voted Miss Congeniality several times over the years. She didn't feel the least bit congenial right now. She felt like she wanted to pop someone in the jaw, and Stella would be smart to turn around and march out the door. "Take it or leave it." Emily glanced at the wall calendar featuring one of their brides from the previous year. "We've got forty-eight hours. After that, cancelling Roselawn will cost me an additional fifteen percent, which means I need a decision by Wednesday at five."

"I'll be in touch." The bride turned on her heel and went out the door with the same hyped-up velocity she'd used coming in. Emily turned toward Allison, sank into the chair next to her desk and wanted to scream. She didn't. Instead she lifted the folder on Allison's desk, made a note and said, "Well. That was fun."

Allison stared at the door, then turned. "Didn't you want to just smack her?"

"Desperately, but not because she was a total in-your-face jerk."

"There was another reason?"

Emily shrugged. "When you do pageants, you have to deal with a lot of drama queens. The problem with this one and this scenario is that I couldn't handle it my way. I had to be nice. I had to schmooze her, and give in, even though it was her mistake. The fact is, we need the money. And that's a situation a lot of folks face every single day of their lives, isn't it? They do the job because they need the money. So." She stood and picked up the folder for a late-afternoon client. "Now it's our turn."

"That's a good point, but I still wanted to smack her."

"I know." Emily frowned at the door. "Mom would have handled her and had her eating out of her hands and paying the extra for the meal and the postage."

"Kimberly would have kicked her."

That made Emily laugh, but she sobered quickly. "Well, she told me to give Stella anything she wanted." She moved toward the stairs, pretty sure she was about the worst party planner ever. "And that's exactly what I did, but I'm real sorry it came to that."

Allison nodded. "Me, too, Emily. But luckily she's the exception in this business. Not the rule."

Was she, Emily wondered? Or had she spotted Emily for a soft touch and behaved accordingly? And if that was the case, having Emily work with difficult clients was going to cost them a whole lot of money, and that spelled disaster. She spent the next two hours angry at herself for not seeing a better way to handle the situation and wishing she didn't have to confess the confrontation to Kimberly when she got back. Her sister had trusted her. She'd just blown that confidence out of the water.

Her office phone rang as she was finishing up the day. She hit Save on a spreadsheet as she reached for the phone. "Thank you for calling Kate & Company. This is Emily."

"Emily, it's Noel Barrister."

Noel Barrister, her former father-in-law and the president of Barrister's Department Stores. He was about the last person she'd expected to hear from, ever. "Noel." She paused and inhaled slowly to calm the adrenaline rush. "This is a surprise."

"I'm sure it is. Do you have a minute?"

She was meeting with a client about a lakeside retirement party in May, but that wasn't until five thirty. "As long as it's brief. I'm expecting a client." *Breathe, Emily. Stay calm.*

Stay cool. They hung you out to dry because their son tossed you aside.

Her heart rate accelerated as memories flooded. She clamped the floodgates down and hauled in a breath.

"I have a business proposition for you. Something that I hope will tempt you back here, to us, but not in Philly. That would be awkward at best, and the last thing I want to make you feel is uncomfortable."

This was quite a change from giving her a nicely padded buyout eighteen months ago, as he showed her to the door the very same day.

"I'd like to talk to you about the New York offices. That way you wouldn't be around Christopher, but you'd be back in the job you loved. A job you excelled at."

And allow them the leverage to fire her again? What was Noel thinking? She *had* excelled at her job; she'd become noteworthy in the short years she'd worked for them, and she still got the boot when his son tossed her aside. "Noel, I don't have time for this right now, but I'm surprised you'd think I'd put myself back into a position where you can let me go with a snap of your fingers on the whim of your son. Why would a rational person do that?"

To his credit, he didn't get defensive. "I'll draw up a contract to ensure that will never happen again. I didn't appreciate what an asset you were to our company, Emily. It's not a mistake I plan to repeat. I'll call you when you have more time, but this will give you something to think about, a buyer's dream. New York City. Fashion Week. The garment district. Fifth Avenue. Just think about it. That's all I ask." He hung up before she could say more.

Noel knew how to push the right buttons, but only a stupid person would trust a Barrister again. She shoved the matter aside as her clients walked in on the lower level. She'd had a rough run-in with her last client. She was determined to have this one go better. It did; the aging couple was charming, and the beautiful bouquet of flowers on her desk reminded her that she hadn't messed up Christa McCarthy's wedding.

Yet.

She walked into Caroline's Bridal the next morning, saw Grant and couldn't control the quick smile. "You beat me here."

"Couldn't wait to see you."

Oh, be still my heart. He was not making it easy to take a firm step back. "If I didn't thank you for the flowers enough yesterday—" she walked right over and surprised him by giving him a hug "—thank you. They brighten the whole office. I love them."

"It was the least I could do. I'm fairly stupid on a regular basis, so this could be the beginning of a trend. I do or say something foolish—"

"Or stubbornly dig your heels in," she added, ever helpful.

"Or insist I'm right when I'm clearly in the wrong." His smile deepened to a grin, and he brought one hand up, skimming her hair, her ear, her cheek. "Flowers are a great apology."

They were a beautiful balm in so many ways, more so after her run-in with Stella. "They made me happy, Grant."

"Well." Warmth filled his gaze. Warmth and joy. "I'm glad, then."

She stepped back as Caroline came toward the front of the cozy bridal store. "Of course, that doesn't mean I'm encouraging bad behavior."

"That would be wrong."

She laughed, and it felt good to laugh with a strong, solid, gentle man. "Yes, it would. Caroline, how are you doing?"

"I'm good, most days, but—" She held out her hands to Emily and frowned. "This arthritis, it is bad now, so bad." She raised her shoulders in a shrug, but her expression indicated she couldn't really shrug this off. "I think the time is near when Caroline's Bridal will become Caroline's retirement. But that is not why you came today." She motioned to the right. "I did as you asked and pulled some gowns, distinct styles from various manufacturers, but I'm going to make a suggestion."

"I'm all ears."

"Good!" She led them toward the bridal rooms. "Christa sent her measurements, her picture and her preferences, what she thinks she likes." She turned to face Emily. "I think it would be good if you were to try on the dresses for her."

"Me?" Emily squawked. "Oh, Caroline, I don't know."

"Well you're here, it's not like I hire models and there's no way that Janet or I can squeeze into any gown Christa might like."

"Well, I—"

Caroline faced her with a frank expression. "If I can give away the gown…"

Ugh. She was right; it shouldn't be a big deal. Emily had modeled before, lots of times in her pageant years. But this was beyond awkward. To try on wedding gowns, in front of Grant?

Her mouth went dry, a silly reaction she needed to get under control. This wasn't about her or her attraction to the handsome highway department supervisor. This was about a dress for a woman serving her country. "Of course I'll do it. It's a great idea, actually."

She didn't look at Grant. She didn't have to. His quiet approval of the situation rang loud and clear when he patted her shoulder.

"Janet will help you in and out of the dresses—my fingers don't have the dexterity to do buttons and lace-up backs anymore. Let's get the first one on because Christa's feed should be coming through in about two minutes. You never know how long an overseas connection might last. When my Justin was deployed, those minutes went all too fast."

"I bet they did." Grant's empathy drew Caroline's smile as Emily entered one of the bridal dressing rooms.

No biggie. She repeated the mantra as Janet zipped her into a simple, formal, strapless gown of cascading chiffon. She walked out of the bridal room, pretending to be casual.

Grant's mouth dropped open.

Emily considered that a win.

She arched a smile his way as she stepped onto the six-inch-high riser in front of a triple mirror just as Christa's voice came through the speaker. "Hey, guys. I'm here."

"Christa." Grant caught sight of her on the screen and looked so excited to see her. He grinned and waved, clearly delighted. "Hey, kid, I miss you!"

"Me, too. A lot," she admitted. "I've got to talk to you, Grant. Tonight, okay? I'm on night duty, so I'll call after the kids are in bed."

"Sure, we can go over everything."

"Perfect." Something in Christa's face said it wasn't perfect, but then Janet fussed with the camera shot to make sure Christa got the best angle on the gowns and the hint of concern disappeared. "This is so nice of you guys. Caroline, Emily, Janet." Christa waved as she spotted them in her laptop screen. "Thank you!"

"You're welcome. Our pleasure," Janet assured her in a too-loud voice, as if the laptop microphone might need help.

"All right, all right, I don't trust these connections, so you two talk while we change Emily in a minute. Christa, hello!" Caroline waved like a crazy woman, right at the camera. "Emily has agreed to try on the gowns, so this first one..." Emily turned, walked, turned and moved as Caroline explained the gown's style, flow and movement. She repeated this with the next six dresses. A fairy-tale-styled gown with gossamer puffed organza sleeves. A mermaid dress, in lace, figure-fitting and snug. Grant's eyes lit up when she walked out wearing that.

"Stunning," he murmured, and there was no missing the appreciation in his gaze.

"Tight," she muttered back.

"Yup."

She sent him a scolding look and was glad when Christa voted that dress out of contention. "I want to be able to move on my wedding day." She laughed. "I spend enough time trussed up with military gear. Beauty and comfort are my only two requisites."

The next dress Emily modeled was vintage lace, with cap sleeves, a heart-shaped back, a fitted bodice and an A-line skirt. Gorgeous, timeless and wearer friendly. Emily gave Christa a thumbs-up when she stepped up onto the riser with Grant's help. "Comfortable, movable, breathable," she told Christa, and the army captain returned the thumbs-up, times two.

"That's the one."

"Really?"

"Yes, it's perfect. Emily, can you turn around?" Emily did, just as their connection wavered, then locked in again. "Yes, this one, definitely. I love it, Caroline, but I'm absolutely insisting on paying for it."

"No you will not. I won't hear of it. This is just a nice way for folks to say thank-you, so you just hush." Caroline faced the decorated air force captain and shook her finger. "You worry about what goes on over there. We've got this covered." She indicated the four of them, her, Emily, Grant and Janet as a crew. "You do your job. Let us do ours. And thank you, Christa Mc-Carthy, to you and Spencer for keeping us safe."

Christa blew her a kiss, and Emily was pretty sure her eyes grew moist. "Thank you, Caroline. Thanks to all of you, I—"

The connection scrambled, then broke, and all they had was a black screen, but that was all right. She'd picked a gown, a beautiful gown. Their goal was met.

As Emily turned to go back into the dressing room with Janet, Grant touched her hand. She turned, and the look in his eyes…

Her heart danced. Her breath caught. He swept her and the dress a long, slow look. "Stunning is right. And I'm not talking about the dress, Em."

"No?" For the life of her, she couldn't bring her voice above a whisper.

"No." He whispered right back, smiling. "I'll go start the paperwork while you get changed."

She wasn't sure if she walked back into that dressing room or floated. Her reflection in the mirror showed flushed cheeks and a happy smile. Janet met her gaze and raised a brow in understanding. "Someone's smitten."

She tried to deny it, then sighed. "Yes. It's silly, right?"

"Love is often silly," Janet told her as she helped her out of the dress. "But in Grant's case, I've prayed a long time for someone to make a difference. He's so alone, more than he realizes. No mother, no sister here, no wife, no faith. Those two little souls, needing so much." Janet lifted her shoulders once she had the gown secured on the broad heavy-duty hanger. "A sweet woman with a love for God and children would be wonderful. I was friends with Dolores for years. She was the kind of mother who went the distance, always, but she was not an easygoing woman. She liked things her way."

Grant had a bit of that quality, too.

"She loved her children," she continued, "and she was in church on a regular basis, helping with this and that, but once you knew her, you realized if Dolores McCarthy said it, she meant it, and there was no changing her mind. And that's not always the best way to do things. Still, for all her hardheaded ways, I miss her like crazy. She would have loved to spoil those twins."

No father, no mother, no wife and his sister deployed. At least Grant had Uncle Percy and Aunt Tillie nearby, with all their old-time eccentricities. Corinne had been a single parent for just over a decade, but her family lived in the area and she was surrounded by Gallaghers at every turn.

Grant didn't have any of that support.

She met Grant up front. He was finishing paperwork with Caroline, and when he saw her moving their way, his eyes—those big gray-blue eyes—brightened.

Caroline slipped out from behind the desk to hug her. "Emily, thank you for helping. That made such a difference to Christa, I'm sure. A gown should always be worn to be appreciated."

"I sure appreciated it." Grant's droll tone raised Caroline's brows.

"A beautiful woman in a wonderful dress is fashion at its best," Caroline declared.

"And on that note." Emily tapped her watch. "I've got to go. I'm overseeing two big events this weekend and if I mess up, Kimberly will kill me. That might not be an exaggeration on my part."

"Knowing your sister, I concur." Caroline paused, flexed her hands, then tried to hide a grimace of pain. "She was a beautiful bride, just lovely. And Drew, a most handsome groom."

"They looked perfect, didn't they?"

"They did," Caroline agreed, but then her voice softened. "Although we all know that marriage is more than how we look on one particular day."

"True words." Grant spoke softly, then extended his hand to Caroline. She stepped back and rebuffed the offer of a handshake.

"I would, Grant, but my hands." She made a face of regret. "Handshakes are painful."

"Then how about this instead?" Grant took hold of Emily's heart when he folded the stout bridal-store owner into a gentle embrace. "Thank you so much for what you did for Christa today. We're both grateful."

His hug made her smile, but Emily wondered how much longer Caroline would be able to hang on to her popular little shop. The sheer weight of some wedding gowns strained the upper body and the hands.

"I'll see you back to the office, Em."

Her phone buzzed. She read *Roselawn* in the display and shook her head. "I hate to say no, but I've got to take this. Caroline, may I use the back office?"

"Of course."

She swept the phone and waved to Grant as she moved down the narrow hall to Caroline's office. She hadn't heard back from Stella, and if Roselawn was calling her, she assumed the angry bride had called them. She sucked a breath and sank into Caroline's seat. "Emily Gallagher, how can I help you?"

"It's Marcia at Roselawn, Emily, and you can start by running interference with your bride."

"Stella?"

"That would be her." Marcia wasn't exactly the warm, fuzzy, happy sort of party house owner. "When we contract with a wedding planner, we expect to work hand in hand with the planner as a liaison and avoid the histrionics I just handled. Ms. Yorkos stormed in here, demanding we give her a price break on her shower because of combined ineptitude on your part and ours."

Could this get worse? Emily knew better than to ask that question, because the Stellas of the world fought for and demanded special treatment. "I offered to have Kate & Company swallow the cost of the additional entrée and resend the invitations."

"Well today's complaint, on top of those, was a pastry table."

If Stella went to Roselawn to demand a pastry table, did that mean she was pulling the wedding shower and wedding or staying with the contract? Emily didn't know. "She's decided she wants one? Because she'd opted out on that when we suggested it."

"She's demanding we provide one at our expense because we should know enough to provide vegetarian choices as a given, not a choice, and that the pastry table will soothe her embarrassment with her peers."

Marcia's words brought a lightbulb moment.

Stella wasn't mad about the entrée, like she claimed. Stella was crazy cheap and wanted to work the angle to get every freebie she could wrangle out of honest business owners. "Marcia, you didn't cave, did you?"

"Not yet, but you know how things are in the winter. We can use the business."

Emily understood her point, but the thought of Stella squeezing special considerations out of people angered her. And when Kimberly returned and found the event messed up, how could Emily justify it? She'd promised Kimberly that all would be smooth for one short week.

It wasn't smooth, and Emily had a wedding and a fiftieth anniversary party to oversee on the coming weekend. Spending extra time soothing Stella's ruffled feathers wasn't how she wanted to spend the next two days, but if Roselawn's call was any indication, she might be doing just that. "I'll talk to her, Marcia."

"Please do. I'm incensed at the idea of giving away a pastry table to serve sixty people, but on the other hand, I don't want those sixty people giving us negative internet reviews. That's a game changer."

"I hear you." Reputation was critical in a popular area like the Finger Lakes. "Let me see what I can do." She hung up as Caroline came down the hall.

"Bad news," Caroline surmised. "Not your dad, is it?"

"A bride."

"Oh. Well." Caroline shrugged. "Emily, there's one thing I've discovered in this business. You win some, you lose some and mostly you make folks happy."

That sounded so delightfully simple.

"Kill 'em with kindness, sweetie. It's much better to smooth back ruffled feathers than to gather them once they've been lost in the wind."

Caroline was right. She needed to bend over backward if necessary to make this right for Stella. And if it cost the business money, she'd make up the difference out of her Barrister buyout account. Dad wouldn't hear of using her settlement money to help pay his medical bills, but if she used it to offset a loss on Stella's wedding, that was her choice.

"I owe you, Caroline!" She hugged the older woman gently. "And I'm going to pray for your arthritis. I am so sorry to see you in pain."

Caroline didn't look up at her. Not at first.

She walked with Emily to the front of the store. Janet was showing a bride around, while four twentysomethings checked bridesmaids' gowns. "The pain's not the hard part. Pills help manage that. It's this." She swept her quaint shop a look. "I love this, I've always loved this and when folks would quack at me to retire, I'd shrug them off. What did they know? But now." Her hands fluttered. "I can't do it."

Emily had seen this same raw emotion in her father's face the previous year, when faced with his prognosis. "Change is hard."

"Yes, it is. I hate to close down, but my options have thinned from narrow to nothing." She clenched her hands, then winced because she'd done it. "I've always told folks to leave things in God's hands, but when it comes to myself, I'm the last to follow my own advice."

"Ain't it the truth?" Emily put an arm around her shoulders. "If you need help with anything…"

"I'll make my firm decision before the busy season starts up again in January, but I think the writing's on the wall. It will break Janet's heart. She's been here a long time, but then, haven't we all?"

Emily's phone signaled a text. Caroline shooed her out the door. "You go on with your day, and when Christa comes into town, you bring her right over. Rita will come in special to do her alterations."

"I will," Emily promised. She checked her phone as she walked south on Center Street. Two texts. One from Noel Barrister, saying he was having a contract drawn up and one from Allison, saying Stella Yorkos had called.

Noel's reminder ignited a flame of temptation back to the garment industry she knew so well. She squelched it, squared her shoulders and called Stella back. "Stella, hello. Allison said you called. How can I help you?"

"You probably can't," the other woman stormed. "You haven't been all that much help so far, but I've been to Roselawn and they're reluctant to try and fix this fiasco of a shower. I'm utterly despondent over this whole ordeal. I can't even think to do my job properly."

Great. Next thing she knew, the savvy and greedy young lawyer would sue them for loss of income. "Well, that's not good, we can't have one of New York's best and brightest unable to work."

"No?"

Emily didn't miss the note of surprise in Stella's voice. "Of course not! We've got the second set of invites done, with the new response cards, and they've been mailed. Also, I talked to Roselawn this morning, and we'd like to offer a complimentary sweets table to your guests to soothe any angst this might have caused. Honestly, Stella, it's the least we can do."

Four distinctly quiet seconds passed. Emily waited, and when Stella said, "Thank you, Emily," in a much more relaxed voice, Emily fist-pumped the air.

"You're welcome. And I know it's an added cost, but you should really think about one for your wedding, as well. Gabriella did one for the Smoltz wedding four weeks back, and I'm still getting calls and reviews, raving about it. When something is that memorable…"

"I'll check it out."

Emily chalked up another success. The Smoltz family was on Stella's guest list, and if April Smoltz's guests loved her wedding, Stella would want to one-up her for sure. "Good. And if you have any questions, Stella, don't hesitate to call me. A holiday-themed shower and a Valentine's Day wedding." Emily paused intentionally to let the unstated appreciative drama mount. "What could possibly be better?"

"Nothing."

Emily scored a mental victory. Yes, her bank account would take a minor hit, but if it kept Stella from badmouthing Kate & Company,

Emily would be okay with that. And if her big sister never found out?

She'd be all right with that, too.

Chapter Nine

Christa's call came through ten minutes after Dolly finally fell asleep. Grant answered the phone and sank onto his favorite recliner. "Hey, nice dress today, Captain."

She laughed. "It's beautiful, Grant. And that was so nice of Emily to model the gowns. This is all so weird, to be doing this halfway across the world."

"But it's coming together," Grant assured her. "You were right, hiring a planner was worth every single penny. And more."

"I'm glad. But that's not why I called, actually."

Something in her voice made Grant sit taller. Straighter. "Then, why? What's up? Are you all right?"

"I'm fine. It's just—" She breathed deep, and then said, "It's Dad, Grant."

"It's what?" He couldn't have heard her right. He hunched forward in the chair, suddenly unrelaxed.

"It's about Dad. I've been talking with him."

Surprise and anger didn't creep up Grant's spine. It raced. "Why? Why would you give him the time of day, Christa? He abandoned Mom, and us. You were a baby, and he walked out on you and never looked back. Why would you think he's important enough to search him out now? Especially with Mom gone."

She kept her voice calm, and that only made him angrier. "What if he did look back, Grant? What if he tried to be part of our lives, but couldn't?"

"The impossibility of that leaves me speechless." Grant stood and ran a hand through his hair, then paced the floor in quick, hard steps. "He didn't have to leave, Christa. And then he didn't have to stay gone. Have you seen him?" He didn't want to ask that question, he didn't want to appear interested. It slipped out because now and again he wondered if his father was even still alive, but never enough to check it out online.

"In Colorado, two years ago. That's where he lives now. He's got a very nice wife, and two kids, Mike and—"

"No. I don't want to hear how I was casually replaced by someone else two thousand miles away. I don't want to hear that he's put his life together with them, while he ignored us. I watched him walk out that door thirty-three years ago, Christa. He kissed me goodbye, told me to be brave and walked away. Mom was crying, you were crying and I was supposed to be a brave five-year-old while my father walked out of our lives." He remembered how he raced to the window and watched as his world fell apart around him. His mother's tears, Christa's baby wails and his father, backing out of the small driveway, onto the road, then driving away.

And he never even looked back to wave.

Oh, he remembered all right, every single second of that horrible afternoon was etched in his brain. "I can't forgive him, Christa. Please don't ask me to."

She sighed and said nothing. Seconds ticked by, long and slow. "Why now, Christa? What's brought this all up?"

"My wedding," she whispered, and the sadness in her tone took Grant by the throat. "Mom's gone, and I'm getting married, and I wanted my father at my wedding. At long last, I wanted a semblance of normal, Grant, but I get it." Her voice firmed. "I really do, and I won't press. I was too young to have any memories, so I have much less to forgive. It's different for you. Way different. But Grant, you should give him a chance to explain."

"Never." He didn't want explanations for why responsible adults walked out on children. He'd lived it twice, and both times he felt like his heart had been ripped from his chest. "Unlike you, I have no desire to reopen those old wounds. I've got enough fresh ones to deal with, thanks. Including two kids who need me to be at my best when we hit the ground running in the morning. I'm calling it a night, Christa." He hung up the phone, then stood, staring at it, filled with disbelief.

She'd gone to meet Joe McCarthy, purposely. Under the guise of vacation, she'd gone out West and arranged to meet their father and his new family. Didn't she understand the pain he put them through? Didn't she get it?

Maybe she's forgiven him, his conscience prodded. *Your mom used to talk about forgiveness all the time, remember? But did she ever forgive your father? Did she ever really move on?*

Grant shoved the mental questions aside.

His mother had worked night and day to care for them. She spent hours each week in church, praying and helping. She was one of those hands-on Christians, always there in a pinch.

Did she ever forgive Joe McCarthy?

Grant didn't care, one way or the other. He checked on Tim and Dolly, sound asleep in their wooden cribs. He couldn't imagine walking out on them.

An image of his former wife came to mind, as she tucked that single picture of Tim on the seat beside her and drove away.

Pain knifed his gut. His chest went tight. He tried to stifle the image, but Christa's talk of forgiveness and reasons kept tugging the memories back.

He couldn't sleep and finally stumbled out of bed at five o'clock, still angry, and now exhausted. He made extrastrong coffee, and when Timmy scrambled down the stairs looking so sweet and innocent in his pajamas, Grant hauled in a deep breath.

He'd get through today on no sleep somehow. And then the next and the next, because that's what a real parent did. They stayed the course, no matter what.

"Emily, you and Allison have done an amazing job." Kimberly handed them each a box of chocolates featuring a fancy emblem on the following Monday.

Emily didn't dare exchange looks with Allison as she accepted the box.

"I had the best honeymoon ever, and I tried not to worry, but—"

"You did worry," Emily filled in from her seat, "hence the fourteen text messages you sent, trying to micromanage from the Caribbean."

Kimberly winced. "Guilty."

"But we managed without you, although I have to say it's really nice to have you back," Emily admitted.

"Your December calendar is free other than Stella's shower and the New Year's Eve gala with me at Chesterton's."

"Yes."

"Time off, well earned."

Emily didn't disagree, but it felt odd, too. In retail, December was a highlight month of sale following sale, doing whatever it took to promote current trends before the January downturn. To *not* be busy felt out of place. She didn't want extra time to think about her failed marriage and career, or her father's prognosis. Being busy would be much, much better.

Her phone buzzed just then. *Grant.*

She smiled, stood and moved down the hall. "Hey, what's up?"

"I'm desperate."

He actually sounded desperate. "What's going on?"

"Mary Flanagan was just taken to a Rochester

cardiac center by ambulance. We've got to pick up all the kids within the hour, but they can't re-open the day care tomorrow with the assistants because they're not certified. We've got snow coming and I love my Aunt Tillie, but she can't watch Tim and Dolly for a whole day, much less however long it takes to get a replacement."

"Poor Mary! Bob's got to be frantic with worry."

"I'm sure he is. And there are only a few day cares in town, and Mary's was the only one willing to take a little one with Dolly's issues."

"Are you serious?" Allison and Kimberly looked up when she raised her tone. "How could a day care facility possibly say no to a child just because they have developmental disabilities?"

"They said they didn't feel equipped."

Equipped? To handle a perfectly wonderful if somewhat stubborn two-year-old? What was so hard about that? Kimberly moved into Emily's line of sight, and pointed to their open December calendar.

Emily met her gaze, nodded, then jumped in, both feet. "I'll watch them."

"What?" Relief and surprise wrapped Grant's tone. "But you're working."

"I've got a light December and Kimberly's back, so there's plenty of time. I'm sure someone will step up to the plate to help Mary out, but until then, I'll watch the kids."

"Em, are you sure?"

Oh, she was sure, all right. The very thought that someone shrugged off a child because they were different made her even more certain. "Absolutely. I'll go pick them up now. Do you have the car seats in your SUV?"

"Yes."

"I'll switch cars with you, then, and go pick them up. We can have an adventure."

"An adventure?"

She ignored the caution in his voice. "I'll be there in ten minutes."

"Em, thank you."

Would he thank her so freely when she took the twins on outings? He'd kept them on a short leash up to this point, but Emily wasn't a short-leash kind of person. She turned toward Kimberly. "You're sure you're okay with this?"

"It's the perfect time," Kimberly assured her. "January will fill with appointments and we have a few winter events, but there's nothing in the next few weeks I can't handle on my own, and we can do the New Year's gala together. Piece of cake."

Just when she'd been ruing having too much time on her hands… "See you later."

"I can't wait to hear how your day goes."

"Fun and getting funner," Emily told her, then dropped her gaze to her dress. "Once I go home and crawl into some jeans, of course."

An email alert came through the phone as she crossed The Square. Noel Barrister, with the word *contract* in the subject line and an attachment icon.

She'd read through that later. Right now, she was off to a twin adventure. She hurried home, got changed and drove to the highway department offices. She walked in, greeted Jeannie and when Grant came out of his office to meet her, she reached out a hand. "Keys, please."

"You're sure you're okay with this?" he asked.

She rolled her eyes.

"And there's not much lunch food for them at home. I figured they'd be at day care so—"

Emily waved him off. "Chicken nuggets, Dad."

"And their nap time is always one thirty to three thirty."

"Or whenever they get tired," she quipped. "Keys."

He handed them over, but didn't cover the look of worry quickly enough. She made a wry face and folded her arms. "They will be just fine. And if you want help with this, I suggest you learn to trust, because if you start second-guessing every little thing I do, then—"

He stood back, hands up, palms out. "You're right, of course."

"She's absolutely right," Jeannie declared from her desk. "These kids are about to have the time of their lives!"

"Yes, they are." She smiled up at him, took the keys and turned. "We will see you tonight, Grant."

"Keep your phone on, okay?"

"Of course." She waved and walked out the door, then drove to Mary Flanagan's. Dolly and Timmy McCarthy were about to have some fun. And so was she. She picked them up from day care, tucked them into their car seats, bought lunch and took the twins to her house. When lunch was done, she bundled them up, clasped a tiny hand in each of hers and took them for a walk around The Square.

People greeted them. Some stopped to chat, while others called out and went on.

The twins stared, shied away and stared again, but by the time she got them back to her driveway, they'd started smiling and waving at people.

She'd heard the forecast of snow that morning, which wasn't a big deal when you walked to work, but two kids and a five-mile trip was a little different. A glance west showed a dark ridge moving their way. She ignored Dolly's protests, changed diapers and tucked them back into their car seats. She texted Grant. Heading to your place before snow.

His text came back immediately. Good!

Grant was a helicopter parent, no doubt about it. Could he relax and take a step back? Life held surprises, but if one trusted in God...

Did Grant trust in God? Did he trust in anything?

Dolly dozed off. Tim fought sleep until she undid his jacket and tucked him into his crib.

She studied their rooms. No sweet pictures of Jesus with children. No Bible passages. No Noah's ark decals or *VeggieTales* friends.

There were eighteen little board books about animals, and not one about baby Jesus.

Could she make a difference in their lives? Or better yet, should she try? She didn't know, and until she knew, she might be smart to keep her defenses up.

Grant wanted to check up on Emily and the kids.

He didn't dare, until the snow hit as predicted late afternoon, and then he called. "Hey, I'm going to be stuck here at least through rush hour. Are you guys home safe and sound?"

"We are." The joy in Emily's voice uplifted him. "I made soup for supper."

"Soup?"

"Mmm-hmm. By the way, two-year-olds don't do well with soup."

He laughed out loud, picturing it.

"Sure, laugh it up. We morphed to PB&J and they're happy as can be. You'll have soup to eat when you do get home. Tillie offered to come over for the night, so you might want to work that out with her."

"She spends the night when snow is predicted so if I get called in, the kids are covered. I'll call her. Emily, I can't thank you enough for today. I'll start scoping out places for them this week and see what's available."

"Kimberly assured me that my presence isn't crucial at Kate & Company this month, so use me as needed. I am helping Rory with the Nativity play at church, so I have to fit their evening practices in. But that's at night, so it shouldn't cause a problem."

"My mother put us in some of those when we were little. I distinctly remember being a shepherd multiple times."

"I bet you were a cute shepherd."

"I expect I was," he drawled and made her laugh.

"The play is in two weeks. You should bring the kids to see it."

"They're two, Emily. They're not going to sit through a play."

"Well, it's short and I think they'd love to see a bunch of other kids doing things. Preschool kids always like to look up to school-age kids. And the music is precious."

Music. More specifically, church music. His mother had helped run so many church events, and she'd played piano for church plays and concerts. Maybe it gave her comfort. He didn't know.

He got nothing out of church. He'd had too many prayers go unanswered. He'd wanted his father back desperately, and oh, how he prayed. He grimaced, remembering. He got nothing, and when his mother fought cancer, she prayed up a storm.

Nothing, again, so Grant was disinclined to waste time pretending. His kids had him, and he'd stand by them forever. "December's busy enough. I have to make time to go shopping and get them in to see Santa. But I'm sure it will go well with you and Rory helping."

"I'm sure you're right." Her tone went from open and friendly to lightly impersonal. "Text me and let me know who's getting here first, you or Tillie. That way I'll let the kids know."

"I will." He ended the call, but stared at the phone before setting it down. Her tone had changed. Why? Because he didn't want to take Tim and Dolly to a play?

A weather alert grabbed his attention, and as he and Jeannie talked to the plow drivers over the radio, he knew he'd be stuck at work for several hours, at least. He was about to call Aunt Tillie, when Uncle Percy walked in and handed him his keys. "Here you go."

"You brought my car into town?"

Percy shook his head. "I dropped the Mrs. at your place to keep an eye on the youngsters, and I followed Miss Emily into town to get her car. She asked me to give you these."

Grant crossed the room and looked out the window. An empty rectangle of pavement stood out in the snow-covered parking lot where Emily's car had been.

She hadn't stopped in or called to let him know she was heading back into town.

He hid his disappointment. He hadn't realized how much he'd looked forward to seeing her at the end of the day, until he didn't.

He pocketed the keys. "Thanks, Uncle Percy."

"Glad to help, and doubly glad not to be drivin' the big rigs in snowstorms anymore. Too many cowboys on the road, not willin' to give a plow room to maneuver. I'll pick Tillie up in the mornin'. Oh, and she said you got a call that Christa's dress came in. Miss Caroline left a message with Tillie, and Tillie said you'd let Christa know."

Christa. The wedding. The angry phone call from the week before. Guilt rose within him. "Of course I will. And thanks for dropping Aunt Tillie off at the house."

"Glad to help." Uncle Percy said it and he meant it. Grant loved that about the aging couple.

"Boss, you okay for the night?" Jeannie pulled her coat and scarf off the wall hooks beyond her desk. "If you are, I'm going to start my car and brush it off so it's thawed out when I'm ready to leave."

He reached out a hand for the keys. "I'll do it. I could use a little fresh air right now."

"I won't refuse an offer like that!" She handed him the keys and motioned to the radio. "I'll keep an eye on things in here."

"I'd appreciate it." He walked into the cold purposely. He'd been downright frustrated since Christa's call the week before. He couldn't get her words or her sorrowed tone out of his head. It ate at him, as if he was in the wrong.

He wasn't. She'd been too little to remember. He remembered everything, in vivid detail. He'd put it all behind him, years ago.

Really? So why are you still angry now?

He didn't know why, but Jeannie's car got the

most thorough brushing he'd ever given. As he rounded the hood, the dusk chorus of church bells began, an old Grace Haven tradition. Bells pealed from three corners of the town, joined by two along Center Street, and then the old stone church began its nightly hymn.

Only this time they didn't play a regular hymn. The tower rang out the plaintive notes of "Taps," a song they played to remember servicemen and women.

Pearl Harbor Day. He'd forgotten the date in his flurry to get the twins cared for. The old church was paying tribute to those who served then, and those who served now.

He thought of Christa, so far away, wishing for family. He'd never been away. He'd lived his entire life in Grace Haven, making a name for himself in his community.

Christa had braved the world, the armed forces and international travel. He remembered pictures of his father in uniform, on the wall. They'd all been taken down when he left, but he remembered them. Father and daughter, both willing to wear the uniform for their country.

The last, drawn-out notes played on the wind. "God is nigh…"

He wasn't. Grant knew that, but the touching notes almost made him wish it was true. He stomped snow off his boots before he walked back into the office and gave Jeannie her keys.

The song talked of all being well.

It wasn't, but was that his fault?

No.

He bit back a sigh as a driver called in. He keyed the microphone. "Grant here." As the driver reported conditions on the southwest perimeter, Grant knew he'd said a mental "no" to accepting any blame, but as the snow continued to fall, he realized his answer should have been "maybe," because three decades was a long time to hold a grudge.

That realization stung.

Lucrative was an understatement for Noel Barrister's contract offer.

Great terms. Amazing benefits. Incredible perks, including wardrobe, and a six-figure salary that meant living in Manhattan wouldn't be a struggle.

Emily stared at her office laptop screen. Her heart thudded in her chest as she reexamined the document.

Noel Barrister wanted her back in the company, badly. The question was why? And was she willing to entertain this offer and resume any kind of relationship with her former in-laws?

The geographical distance and the no-fire

clause inside a buyout option made her realize this offer could be a genuine possibility. She picked up her phone and dialed his number. It was after hours, but Noel wouldn't care about that. He and Christopher's grandfather hadn't grown Barrister's to a five-state chain without putting in the time. He answered on the second ring.

"Emily, good to hear from you. My offer arrived, I take it?"

"It did, and it's quite generous."

"As promised."

"Yes, again. But why, Noel?" She leaned back in her chair and put her feet up. "What's happened? And please just tell me outright—spare me the trouble of digging up current figure comparisons to twenty-four months ago."

"You answered your own question. Sales jumped appreciably when you were in charge of women's clothing. They've dropped by double digits this year, and that's a wake-up call. Not everyone sees how things will look. You do. It's a gift and you have it."

She did. She understood body types, styles and fabrics. There was a science to putting the puzzle pieces together, but did she love it enough to work for a Barrister again?

The offer tempted her forward.

Common sense held her back. "You understand that I need to stay here for several months still. My father is undergoing cancer treatments, and I can't leave my sister in a lurch."

"Unacceptable." Noel clipped the word. "And no parent in their right mind would expect their child to miss an opportunity like this. Time is money, Emily. Always was, always will be. I'd need you here by mid-January at the latest."

"That's quite impossible, so let's end this call amicably. Goodbye, Noel."

"February first." He barked the words and sounded pained to do so. "That's eight weeks away. I cannot believe that your sisters can't handle the business on their own come February. It's illogical to think otherwise."

Could they?

Rory wasn't a fan of weddings and event planning, and Kimberly was rock solid in the industry, but they'd booked a lot of events for the coming year already. With her mother retiring, should she assume a place in Kate & Company? Or move on?

"Train someone, for pity's sake. Companies do it all the time."

He was right, but that wasn't the question. The question lay within her. Did she want to stay? Or go? Did she belong here or there? "I'll take it under consideration."

"I can't wait forever, Emily."

"Noel, your impatience won't gain favor with me. You've extended a professional offer. I will make a professional decision once I've had a chance to examine it. I'll be in touch soon."

He hung up without saying goodbye, probably miffed that she didn't jump aboard immediately.

She shrugged into her coat and scarf, turned off the lights and walked out the front door of Kate & Company.

Church bells sounded as she put the key in the lock.

She loved their joyful call to evening, the co-operative work of several churches, and when the old stone church began playing "Taps," she sighed at the beauty of the music, the snow and the night.

Could she stay and be around Grant and not grow to care too deeply for him? Did she dare? Or would she be smarter to cut her losses and start anew?

The disciple Peter talked about being sober and watchful in his Biblical letters. He warned that evil prowls like a roaring lion.

Was the lure of money calling her? Or was it the chance to succeed in her chosen career? Or both? And if both, was that wholesome?

Questions dogged her. She paused by the town gazebo, the very spot where Kimberly and Drew had stood for wedding photos, and she gazed around.

Let go and let God. Trust, Emily. Put your trust not in yourself or others, but in Him.

Her mother's words were the reminder she needed now and again.

The snow started falling harder. Thicker. Already it blanketed the ground. The heavy-duty grind of a snowplow engine brought Grant to mind.

Let go and let God.

Her mother was right, and for the moment, Emily needed to do exactly that. She walked home through the quickly mounting snow, grabbed a shovel from the garage and began clearing the walk.

It would fill up again, as long as the snow continued, but doing something manual felt good. And when the walks were fully cleared, the thought of a warm house seemed real nice. She turned to go in just as Grant's SUV rolled up the driveway.

Her heart sped up.

She ordered it to stop that nonsense, right now.

Her heart had other ideas. When he climbed out of the car and crossed the drive, the sight of him, rugged and strong, dressed in working man's clothes, pulled at her.

"You're shoveling?"

"Just finished."

"I'd have done this for you." He reached out and tucked her hair back, behind her ear, then indicated the walks with his gaze, but didn't move his hand. "It would be my pleasure, Em."

The strength of his callused hand against her cheek, against her ear sent warmth through her. "Grant, I—"

"You're beautiful with snowflakes in your hair." He spoke softly, tenderly. "But you're beautiful without the snowflakes, too."

"Grant..."

"Em, I'm not sure what you see in me." He put two warm hands against her cool cheeks and shrugged lightly. "I'm stubborn, maybe even bullheaded, and I'm not even close to perfect, but when I look at you, I want to be more perfect. To be a better person. And right now..." He stopped talking and shifted his gaze from her eyes to her lips. "Right now..."

She lifted her chin and that was all the permission he needed. He dropped his head and his lips met hers.

Perfect.

Perfectly matched, perfectly marvelous.

He kissed her sweetly, as snow fell on and around them, a winter's hush on the land, the town. And when he deepened the kiss, Emily's heart wanted nothing more than to be in this man's arms.

"Em." He whispered her name when he gathered her into a long, warm embrace, the kind of hug a woman would cherish forever. "I know this shouldn't have happened. I know you're planning on leaving when things get right, but I had to know."

"Know what?"

"If kissing you would be just as wonderful as I thought it would be. And the answer is yes. It was. Now what are we going to do about it?"

The softness of his leather collar warred with the late-day bristle on his cheeks and chin. The combination of falling snow, warm hugs and sweet, tender kisses wiped any semblance of rational thought from her brain. "Kiss some more and figure things out in the reality of daylight?"

He laughed and obliged most willingly, then hugged her close again. "I've got to get home. We've got lake-effect bands that are going to kick into gear the next few weeks, but just thinking about those kisses will keep me going, Em."

Beautiful kisses. Beautiful children. A fairy-tale kind of life in so many ways.

But life was more than fiction. She reached her hand up to his cheek. He turned his face and kissed her palm.

"I'll see you in the morning, okay?" She

stepped back because if she didn't, she might linger in the yard forever, lost in the moment.

"Okay."

He started toward the car, and when he turned and lifted his hand in farewell, she did the same. "God bless you."

"Good night, Em."

No sweet blessings at the McCarthy's. No grace before meals, nothing faith based.

Conflicted, she watched as he pulled away.

Noel, and his gruff, no nonsense, take-no-prisoners offer.

Grant, a man she cared for, who shrugged off God as a nonentity.

Let go and let God.

She put the shovel away, walked up the sidewalk and let herself in. If this was a test, one way or another she was determined to pass it. She'd pray for wisdom and discernment, because emotion alone couldn't win the day.

She'd done that once, and Emily Gallagher never wanted to make a serious mistake about marriage or life again.

Chapter Ten

❧

Grant looked sleep deprived when she arrived at his house the next morning. The twins, however, looked well rested and raced to greet her. She bent low, arms wide. "Hello, Munchkins! Are you ready for days of great adventure? To boldly go where no toddler has gone before, my darlings?"

Dolly screeched and patted her cheek in excitement. Timmy latched on to her leg and refused to let go, so she plunked herself onto the kitchen floor and let them explore her.

"Hug!" Timmy launched himself into her arms and when he drew himself back, he laughed right into her face. "More hug!"

"I could hug you all day, my little gingersnap!"

"I love gingersnaps." Grant stood by the table, looking down at them. Mixed emotions deepened the fine lines around his eyes. "And playing with these two. Wish I could stay and have fun with all of you."

A part of her wished that, too. Being with him and the kids put her in a state of longing. But she was a baseball lover from way back when her brother and Drew played Legion ball. Three strikes was a firm out in any league. Grant was unforgiving, overprotective and didn't believe in God. "Well, someone has to be the wage earner, which means you go to work." She motioned to the table. "My keys are right there. And we stay here and plan our day!"

"About that…"

"Yes, Grant?" She challenged him by locking eyes with him, then asked smoothly, "Do you need my driving credentials? You can have Drew run my license to check for tickets and violations."

He looked downright uncomfortable.

Good.

Grant McCarthy was used to his word being law at the office, in the town and in his house.

But not with her.

She extricated herself from the floor, and when he offered a hand up, she took it and found herself up close, next to him.

Sparks hummed between them. No, not sparks, bolts. Lightning-sized bolts of sweet attraction.

Her hand in his, their arms together, touching. Close enough to feel him breathe and want to share that breath. Close enough to sense his emotions and want to calm them or maybe rile them even more.

He squeezed her hand softly. He bent, just a little, to hold her gaze, and for the life of her, she couldn't look anywhere else. "Thank you, Em."

Kindly words of gratitude. He smiled then, a slow, broad smile, the kind of smile that needed no words. "I'll see you tonight."

"We'll be here."

He released her hand, but she was pretty sure he didn't want to release her hand. He dropped his keys on the table and pocketed hers.

Victory.

"Bye, guys." He stooped and gave the twins each a kiss and a hug. "Daddy loves you. Be good, okay?"

"Wuvs you, wuvs you, wuvs you!" Timmy jigged around the kitchen to imaginary music. "See you, Dad!"

"Will do, big guy. Bye, Doll-face."

Dolly grinned up at him, silent, sure that was enough.

Emily crouched down. "Say bye-bye."

Dolly grinned harder.

"The smile's super cute, kid, but words are where it's at. Say bye-bye."

Dolly nodded to say she understood, and said nothing.

"It's okay," Grant said. "Her smile says it all."

Emily stood, reached up and grabbed hold of his jacket to get his attention.

Oh, it got his attention, all right. For a moment he seemed to think she was going to kiss him goodbye, and the thought crossed her mind, but that wasn't why she made the move. "Stop babying her."

He flushed.

"If she needs to be pushed to learn things that help her fit into society, then we push. Got it?"

He could have gotten angry. He could have been put out by her sass and her tough-girl attitude, but he wasn't, because his hand came up, his big, strong, beautiful right hand, and he laid it against her face, cupping her cheek. "You said *we*."

He held her gaze with his, dropped his gaze to her lips, then settled a light kiss against her mouth. It was soft and strong all at once, the kind of kiss a girl dreams about and rarely experiences. She couldn't move if she wanted to, and moving was the last thing she wanted to do. "I love the sound of that word, Em."

He caressed her cheek gently and smiled. "See you later."

"Okay." One word was all she could manage. When was the last time a kiss rendered her speechless?

She couldn't remember, so that was either a very bad sign or a really good one.

A sudden crash brought her back to reality. *Don't turn your back, because destruction can and will ensue.*

She popped Dolly into a high chair, latched the tray firmly in place, gave her a big crayon and white paper to amuse her while Emily cleaned up the half gallon of spilled milk and a generous shaking of cereal.

She wasn't here to win Grant's heart or to give hers. She was here to do a good service to these sweet kids.

But that kiss...

She didn't dare close her eyes and relive the kiss because then nothing would get done. She fed the kids, turned on the TV when they were done eating and did a quick kitchen cleanup. By ten o'clock, the kitchen was in decent shape, everyone had a fresh diaper and the SUV was warming in the garage. She packed the double stroller and took the twins to the play center in the big mall in Victor. They climbed, they ran, they laughed.

By noon, she was on the road again. She cruised through one drive-through for coffee and another for chicken nuggets, then decided to surprise Grant with a submarine sandwich from the Italian deli just off Center Street. She called and placed the order, but when she pulled into their parking lot, she realized her quandary. No drive-through.

Oops.

Getting the kids in and out for a one-minute pickup made no sense, so she called the deli from the car, explained her predicament and when GiGi DiTucci hurried outside with her order and change for a twenty-dollar bill, Emily hugged her. "Thank you so much!"

"This is what small towns do." GiGi waved to the twins, excited to see them. "They help one another. Go with God, Emily!"

"And you, GiGi. Thank you!"

She pulled out of the deli's lot and drove over to the Grace Haven town highway department offices. Grant McCarthy was about to be surprised.

His kids were mobile. Grant wasn't too sure what to make of the news. On one hand, he trusted Emily.

The other hand, the one that had been rocking cradles on its own for over two years, wanted control. He was pretty sure that side was about to lose the battle.

Sara from the coffee shop called to tell them how adorable the twins were and how they waved to her from the backseat.

GiGi called exclaiming about how big they were getting.

And Martha Bryant called to say how she enjoyed running into them at the mall. All this and the clock had just struck twelve. He wasn't sure if he should be overjoyed or worried sick, but when Emily came breezing into the outer office with kids and lunch, his heart leaped the instant he laid eyes on her with Timmy and Dolly.

"Hey." He came out of his office, picked Timmy up and smothered him with kisses. "What a nice surprise."

"Oh, you precious bundles!" Jeannie bent low and smiled into Dolly's eyes. "How are you, darling?"

Dolly's face started to crumple, but when Emily said "Uh, uh," Dolly paused and looked up. She gulped, and her lower lip quivered, but she didn't make a fuss.

Grant was amazed and proud, and decided he liked that a whole lot better than apologizing for Dolly's regular outbursts.

Emily smiled down at her. "Much better! Good girl, Dolly. Can you say hello?"

"Wo."

Grant stared, then lifted surprised and grateful eyes to Emily. "She said it."

"She did. We're going to work on diction and pronunciation. She needs to work harder to make her tongue form the sounds, but hard work wins the day, doesn't it, Doll-face?"

Dolly smiled when Emily palmed her head of curls. "Wo! Wo!"

"You are so good with her." Sincerity marked Jeannie's compliment. "You probably don't remember me, but I used to cheer you on at local pageants. I'm Jeannie Delgado."

"Your son Bob was in my graduating class."

"He was." Jeannie looked pleased that Emily remembered. "I think he had a crush on you for years."

Grant lifted his chin, because Bob Delgado was a single young executive, living in nearby Rochester, and he had no business being interested in Emily. Then or now.

"The sweetest tribute there is," Emily declared. "Tell him I said hi."

"I will."

Emily turned his way and lifted the shopping bag. "Have you eaten yet?"

He hadn't even thought of food yet, and the smell of seasoned deli meat made his mouth water. "I thought you didn't like cold cuts."

She shook her head. "I can't look at cold cuts. If someone else makes me a sandwich, with no personal contact on my part, then I can eat them. And GiGi's subs are to die for, but I didn't get one for me. I'm cooking for Rory tonight, so I need to save an appetite for later, but I got one for you and nuggets for the kids. I thought we might be able to have a carpet picnic."

"A what?" Did he look as out of his element as he felt right now?

"A carpet picnic. Like on the floor of your office."

"Kids eating on the floor?"

She strolled right past him and into the office. "Come here, darlings."

Timmy scrambled to get down. Dolly followed along as fast as she could, hands out, clearly in love with her new day care provider, and why shouldn't she be? In one morning Emily had taken the initiative to get them out of routine. Dolly's occupational therapist had suggested this often. Grant had been adept at ignoring the idea. Home was comfortable, safe and secure. Less chance for Dolly to fall or be hurt, and easier to control her fits of temper. Was it bad to want them safe?

Not bad, he realized as the toddlers plopped down onto the worn carpet. Just stifling, and *that* was bad. "We're really going to sit on that floor? Where workmen come in wearing boots and tromping snow and salt?"

"These are all natural compounds found everywhere we go this time of year, and clearly it's been vacuumed recently. We're going to sit here." She followed that by taking a seat on the floor, using the tacky black vinyl couch as a backrest. "You can proceed as you wish. The white bag is yours."

He opened the bag. "A grandfather sub."

She grinned. "You like?"

"I haven't bought one of these since summer when we were rebuilding the runoff swales for the Clowden development."

"The new neighborhoods being built off Hunter Road."

"Yes."

"That's a great area," she told him. When he took a seat next to her, her smile was enough of a reward. "Pretty houses, nice yards, at least in phase one and two, and filled with kids because it's affordable to normal people."

"How do you know all this?"

"Drew and Kimberly were house hunting over there. Although I'm a big fan of village houses."

"Because you were raised in the village?"

She shrugged. "Maybe. I love being able to

walk all over. To work, for food, for friends, shopping...and church."

"There is a major convenience when you live in town," he admitted. "If you like people."

"I do."

He winced. "I know. I'm kind of stuck on privacy, myself."

"Ah."

He'd failed a test. He knew it, but he couldn't pretend to be something he wasn't. Could he?

His mother used to tease him about being a stick-in-the-mud. Was he? Was he that married to his own choices?

"Although being in a neighborhood with the right person could make all the difference." He took a bite of his sandwich, one of the best sandwiches he'd ever had, and waited to see what she'd say as the kids gobbled chicken nuggets and apple slices.

"It could." She paused, and Grant began to understand the seriousness of her words. "But to deliberately put yourself or others in a situation they don't or won't like wears folks down after a while. That can't be healthy for a relationship."

Like Serenity.

She'd changed the rules of the game, deciding she didn't want children several years into their marriage. And years later, when she discovered she was pregnant, she continued the pregnancy for him. He hadn't thought of that as sacrificial, before. It was what mothers did, wasn't it? Now he glimpsed the reality behind her choice, and he surprised himself. "I thought being a grown-up would be a piece of cake. You make your own rules and follow them. It didn't exactly work out that way, and it's hard sometimes."

"It is, isn't it? And yet." She swept the twins a quick look, a look so sweet and filled with humor and appreciation that Grant's heart pushed open a little wider still. "Being a grown-up gives us amazing opportunities."

"Dowwy, dat's mine!" Timmy reached across his sister to reclaim his apple slice. "Gimme, Dowwy!"

Quick as a wink, Dolly stuffed the apple slice into her mouth.

"She'll choke." Grant moved to help her, but Emily paused him.

"She's fine, just greedy." She picked Dolly up and put her on the couch. "You don't take Timmy's food. That's naughty."

Dolly scowled, chewed and swallowed, then scowled again.

"Sit. You're in time-out."

"Oh!" Timmy's eyes grew wide. "Dowwy's in time-out! Dowwy's naughty!"

"She won't stay," Grant whispered. "I don't think she comprehends the idea."

"Hush."

He drew back.

If anyone else took charge like that, he'd have chafed. With her, he didn't half dare, maybe because she was often right. Or because she was one of the sauciest, nicest, most beautiful and kindhearted people he'd ever met.

Dolly started to climb down.

Emily put her right back on the couch and tapped her watch. "Two minutes."

Dolly frowned and repeated her action.

So did Emily.

By the third time, Grant was pretty sure his daughter was going to explode.

She didn't. She faced Emily, stared, then folded her arms and made a grumpy face and sat, right there, until Emily told her to get down.

"You got her to do it."

"Of course I did. Every kid needs structure, and kids with limitations need it just as much, if not more. It builds a trust relationship over and above the love relationship."

"My mother was like that. Strong and firm, but nice."

Emily laughed. "I'm not sure that's a good thing, that I remind you of your mother, but if she stood her ground with a stubborn boy like you, more power to her."

He laughed, too. "I gave her a run for her money, no doubt. She never played games or changed the rules midstream."

"It's hard to win the game when the rules change." She put a soft hand to his sleeve. "But God gives us second chances all the time. When someone closes a door, God opens up a window."

"Sunday school logic." He didn't sound overly impressed.

"And everyday life," Emily said lightly. She stood and started cleaning up the twins' mess. "We've got to bug out."

"Bug!" Timmy screeched the word, looking around.

"Bug?" In contrast, Dolly looked curious.

"Sorry, Timmers, there's no bug. Can you throw this away for me, please? Grant, where's your trash can?"

"Next to my chair."

"There we go." She steered Timmy in the right direction and he became a boy on a mission. He threw away their wrappers and cartons, and tried to throw away his sippy cup and Grant's sandwich.

"Such a good helper!" Emily swung him up as Dolly pushed to her feet. "I think we'll spare

Daddy's sandwich and we'll keep the cup, okay, my friend?" She held up her hand and he high-fived her.

"Okay!"

"Me, me, me!" Dolly held up her hand for a high five, too. Grant gave her one and she beamed. "Dowwy good, Dowwy good, Dowwy good."

"Two-word sentence, excellent, my smart little friend." Emily fussed over her as if she'd just delivered a valedictorian address. "Well done, Dolly!" She kissed Dolly's cheek while she helped Tim into his jacket. "Dude, you need to learn how to do this yourself. That will be tomorrow's lesson. Give Daddy a hug and kiss goodbye, okay?"

"I'll help you out to the car." He was all set to argue his point, sure she'd say no, but she surprised him.

"Oh, that would be lovely."

It was lovely. Being with her, eating with the kids, the surprise visit, her spunk, her charm.

She's bossy and you will never get a bit of rest.

He grinned to himself, liking the sound of that. She was bossy. She knew her own mind. She wasn't afraid to challenge the status quo, where he was generally determined to live the norm.

She shook him up and he liked it, most of the

time. He took Dolly's hand and walked her to the car. The wind had kicked up, and the expected snow squall had barreled in off the lakes. "You okay to drive in this?"

"In snow?" She looked around as if not sure she heard him right. "I think when you've lived in upstate most of your life, you either learn to drive in snow, or you live a very sedentary life."

"I hear you. I'll stop fussing."

"Good."

He smiled at her. "Thank you for surprising me."

She lifted one shoulder. "It's good to keep men on their toes. Surprises in life are a welcome diversion."

"I concur. I found myself singularly diverted this morning, Emily."

Color stained her cheeks. "See you later."

"Will do."

She climbed into the driver's seat, and he watched as she pulled away, unmindful of the snow and wind.

Her presence made him want to do better. And the difference in Timmy and Dolly amazed him. He was sorry Mary Flanagan was stricken, really sorry, but he was happy to have Emily with his children. He went back to work and ate his sandwich as he plotted line-item budget concerns for the next town meeting and had one of the best afternoons he could ever remember.

Best week ever, Emily decided on Friday.

She took the twins on several field trips, she played, she taught, she read and she snuggled sweet, sleepy toddlers midafternoon. Dolly continued to show progress, and Tim was less incensed by his stubborn, naughty sister.

It was a beginning, but to what end? She tucked them in for their Friday naps and went back to the kitchen, unsure how to answer that question.

Her phone rang on the granite countertop. Noel's name and number flashed in the display. "Noel, hello."

His voice came through sure and crisp, like always.

"Just checking in. We're in the middle of typical holiday frenzy, but I wanted to touch base with you. Have you had your lawyer go over the contract as yet?"

"I've emailed it to her."

It almost sounded like he breathed a sigh of relief. "That means you're considering the offer."

"I'm keeping my options open at the moment," she told him, "but on *my* time frame. If that's unsatisfactory, we can quietly end the discussion right now." She'd learned the hard way that if Noel got an inch, he demanded a mile.

"December is no time for Barrister's to change anything at corporate level, and you know that, but I need a definite answer by mid-January at the very latest." He kept his tone brisk, no-nonsense. "You know this business, Emily. You have the younger and more empathetic eye we need to court customers of all ages. I was stupid to let you go, and I'd like to rectify that lapse in judgment."

Noel Barrister called himself stupid?

She paced the floor, phone in hand, surprised. "I'll have an answer for you by then."

"Good." He hung up without saying goodbye, another annoying trait.

Like a skilled fisherman, Noel was tempting her back into the game she'd loved. And the New York City office was a power seat, but was that still her dream? Or had her goals changed since being home?

Tillie arrived to relieve her while the twins were still napping. She called Roselawn from her car phone to double-check arrangements for Stella's shower the following day. They went over the list together, and everything seemed in order. Would Stella see it the same way?

Time would tell.

She promised Marcia she'd arrive early and got home as the six o'clock bells started pealing.

There would be no chorus of church bells in Manhattan. There would be no GiGi dashing out to her car in the snow, happily handing her change. No Grant and no twins. But what was love without shared faith? An empty vessel, never full.

There were no perfect answers in her life right now. January was short weeks away. She'd made a promise to her parents, but she understood the reality. Kimberly could handle running the business with Allison. From this point on, with much of the coming year booked and secured, she wasn't really needed at Kate & Company.

And that meant the decisions were firmly back in her hands.

Chapter Eleven

Emily was thirty-five minutes into Stella's wedding shower. Food was about to be served and she was almost ready to breathe easy.

The Victorian motif dining room was awash in twinkle lights and red and white poinsettias, in keeping with Stella's holiday theme. Marcia and the staff had outdone themselves in laying out a perfectly beautiful afternoon. Nothing could possibly go wrong.

"I can't believe you did this, Stella!"

The small chorus of voices near Emily paused. So did she, because suddenly she wasn't breathing all that easy anymore. She turned toward the angry voice. So did everyone else.

"You did it on purpose, you selfish witch, and I regret the day I said yes for Katelyn to be in your self-absorbed, egotistical wedding, but that's a mistake I can remedy right now! If only

I could convince my brother." The somewhat stout woman stepped closer. Anger and hurt darkened her gaze while a single tear tracked down her cheek. She brushed it away. "That you are the most self-centered person I've ever met in my life. Be assured that my family will not be in or at your stupid wedding. An adult shouldn't have to deal with your behavior, much less a sweet child like Katelyn."

What could Emily do? She had no idea what had transpired, and the entire room was now focused on the emotional scene playing out before them.

Tears streamed down the six-year-old's cheeks. Her mother grabbed tissues and their coats, then stormed out of the festive room.

Shocked silence settled in her wake.

But in that shocked silence, Emily saw Stella's face. She didn't look like a bridezilla right now. She looked like an overwhelmed woman. Her expression changed quickly, though, as the room rumbled back to life.

"Stella, how dare she?" Mrs. Yorkos hurried to her daughter's side. "This is what comes from marrying into that kind of family—"

About 25 percent of the room gasped. Emily guessed those were members of the groom's family.

"Mother!"

"It's true," Yvonne Yorkos insisted. "Your father's family, my family, we have standards!"

Half a dozen people started for the door.

"In the old days, you'd have never married beneath you like this!"

Another dozen followed.

Stella's mother whirled around, saw people leaving and seemed to realize that she had just managed to insult a quarter of the guests.

The groom's mother approached them. "Yvonne, really. Think about what you're saying, please."

Mrs. Yorkos planted her hands on her hips and scowled. "You know it's true, Deborah. In our day, a young woman from Brant Hills wouldn't have given the time of day to a farmer's son."

"Mom!" Stella moved between the two women, and for once she had the grace to look appalled. "Scott is a great man, he's doing wonderful things for the county and he'll probably end up being a state congressman. Or a senator. What are you doing?"

"Clawing one's way up is never the same as being born up, Stella, and Deborah knows the truth in my words."

The other mother didn't look angry. She looked sad, and she put a gentle arm around Stella's shoulders. "Yvonne, I know that you believe your words. But look around you. You're the only one in this room who believes them. Times have changed, and while I'm not feeling particularly welcome here at the moment, I want Stella to know that she's my son's choice as his bride. His helpmate for life. And I welcome her to our family." She kissed Stella's cheek, then joined the rest of the people walking out the door. In less than five minutes, a group of just over sixty people had been cut to forty.

Silence reigned.

Stella stood, facing the door, wringing her hands, as if she couldn't believe what just happened. Two bridesmaids came forward. The other two hung back. Emily understood their reluctance because there were no reassurances to fix this.

"Stella." She moved to the bride's side and took her arm. "Let's make sure the remaining guests enjoy their afternoon."

Stella met her gaze, then swallowed hard. Tears slipped down her cheeks.

Marcia appeared with a box of tissues. She proffered them, and Emily handed several to Stella. "We can do this." She kept her voice soft. "Families squabble all the time, and everyone here understands that you are your own person, and Scott's bride. Give things time to calm down, okay?"

Stella blinked, then nodded.

Emily took her arm, then motioned for Marcia to start serving. Food wouldn't change anything, but she hoped it would create a buffer. And then presents.

Talk about awkward.

Every time Stella was handed a gift signed by her future in-laws, the guests exchanged not-so-furtive glances and Stella looked miserable.

Worst wedding shower, ever.

That's how this one was getting labeled in Emily's book, and if she never had to deal with a cranky bride again—

She'd be okay with that.

Grant picked up his ringing cell phone Monday afternoon and couldn't believe what he saw. His ex-wife's maiden name and a number he didn't recognize. The phone buzzed three times before he swept a finger across the touch screen. "Grant McCarthy speaking."

"It's Serenity, Grant."

"It's been a long time, Serenity."

"It has. I know. I…" She paused, then said, "I'd like to see you, if that's all right."

"Me? You want to see me?"

"Yes."

"Not your children?" He asked the question

purposely as anger rose within him. "You have no interest in seeing them?"

"Why confuse them?" The words came through soft, so soft. He had to grasp the phone tighter to his ear to hear them. "I'm in the area for a little while and I wanted the chance to clear up some things."

Clear up what? How she walked out and left her two babies? "I don't see any sense in it, Serenity. What's the point?"

She sighed. A long silence ensued before she spoke again. "You're right, of course. There really is no point." She hung up the phone and he sat there, staring at it, the sight of her name engraved on his brain.

Why had she called now? She'd taken off a long time ago. Why contact him now and ask to see him?

She didn't want to see their kids.

Well, she didn't *deserve* to see their kids. She didn't deserve their love and affection and silly ways, and sleepless nights and messy diapers. He'd been there night and day. He'd walked the halls with croupy kids and upset tummies and stuffed-up noses and sore gums from teething. Him, not her, so she could—

"Grant, I'm heading out. Have a good weekend."

Jeannie's goodbye interrupted his mental tirade. He stood, shrugged off the call and moved to grab his jacket, scarf and gloves. "You, too."

"See you tomorrow. And I hope the storm they're forecasting either gives us a miss or weakens before it hits New York. Getting to work might be a tricky business."

"If it hits, I'll get the guys out in plenty of time to clear things up."

She sent him a fond look. "You're good at your job, Grant. The whole town appreciates that. You remind me a lot of your mom. Always helping, ready to take charge."

"Thanks, Jeannie." He locked the doors once he shut off the lights, and trudged to his SUV, chin down.

He couldn't believe Serenity called him out of the blue like that. Why? What good would talking do? What good could come of it?

None.

He climbed into the SUV, determined to put Serenity and the phone call behind him. He and the kids were doing fine, and no way did they need a wrinkle in the road to mess things up. Even if that wrinkle was their mother. She'd shrugged them off and walked away, and never looked back.

His conscience gave him a solid poke. *She's looking back now. Isn't that why she called?*

He didn't know and didn't care. He drove

home. Tillie was finishing out the final hour with the twins because Emily had a client appointment.

He walked in and hugged his kids, hugged them tight. He loved them. He'd do anything for them. And no matter what happened, he'd be here for them, all the time, because that's what a good parent did. He cared for the kids all evening, trying to shove thoughts of Serenity aside, but they kept budging in.

First Christa with their father. And now Serenity, pushing in.

Well, that wasn't how it worked, Grant thought as he tucked the twins into bed a few hours later. There were no free passes in life. Life with kids was like the famous Yoda saying—"Do. Or do not. There is no try."

His father left without a backward glance. Serenity walked out on two infants to pursue a career she loved more than them.

And that was it, Grant decided when he punched his pillow into shape late that evening. If asked, he'd say he believed in second chances, sure. But not when it involved the tender hearts of children. Then you got one shot to make it right, and if you blew it?

The game was over.

He went to bed, exhausted, but sleep was a long time coming. He must have dozed, though, because he sat straight up in bed hours later, jerked awake by what?

He listened hard, heard nothing and was tempted to lie back down. The clock read 3:47. He checked his cell phone. No weather alert or anything to call the crews out for. He yawned, eyed the pillow and decided to check the kids before he went back to sleep.

He peeked into Dolly's room. Sound asleep, curled up tight, eyes buttoned shut, she looked strong but frail. Was that because he saw her limitations and not her strengths?

Possibly, and he needed to work on that. Heaven knows Emily reminded him on a regular basis.

He moved to Timmy's room and opened the door. The sound of Tim's breathing yanked him into the room, and when he clicked on the light he knew something was wrong, very wrong. "Tim?" He picked up the boy, speaking softly. "Timmers? It's me. Daddy."

No response, just that awful labored breathing as if his little boy was struggling for air.

Panic rose.

He fought it down.

He'd handled lots of illnesses with the kids, but never anything like this. "Timmy? Timmy, wake up, honey. Wake up, okay?" He stared at the little fellow, as if the heavy breathing might remedy itself once Timmy woke up, but the sight of Timmy's blue-tinged lips made his decision easy and hard. He carried the boy back to his room, grabbed up his phone and made two calls. The first was to 911, to report a child with trouble breathing.

And the next was to Emily Gallagher.

Emily grabbed for the phone. "Grant, what's up? What's wrong?"

"It's Tim." He was trying to sound calm, but the fear in his voice grabbed hold of her heart. "The ambulance is on its way to take him into the children's hospital at Strong."

"Why?"

His voice cracked. "He's sick. He's having a hard time breathing. His lips are turning blue, Em."

God, oh, God. Please shelter this little boy and his father. Heal him, Lord—shed Your healing mercy upon him like the dewfall, all encompassing. Heal him, Lord. Please. "You'll have to come through town to get to the thruway. Meet me at the corner of Center and Lake Road and I'll take Dolly."

"You don't mind?"

"Of course I don't." She heard the sound of the approaching ambulance coming through

Grant's phone and her heart seized. "I'll grab her so you can focus on him, okay?"

"Yes."

Rory came into her room as Emily quickly tugged clothes into place. "What's going on?" When Emily explained, Rory stepped up to the plate, like always. "I'll take Dolly. You go with Grant. He shouldn't be alone at a time like this."

Emily's car was freezing cold, but by the time Grant pulled up to the intersection a couple of blocks from the Gallagher house, it had warmed up. Emily climbed out. So did Rory. And when Rory took Dolly and the spare booster seat, Emily got into the passenger seat of Grant's car. "I'm coming with you."

He covered her hand with his for just a moment, but it was long enough. "Thank you, Em. I—" He breathed deep, thrust the car into gear and headed for the thruway. "I can't believe this is happening. He was fine last evening. Just fine."

"And fine yesterday, although he did seem tired at nap time. More tired than usual, but we'd played hard all morning."

"I don't get it." Grant went through the toll-booths a few minutes later, accelerated and took the next exit, toward Rochester. "How can a kid be perfectly healthy one minute and struggling to breathe the next?"

"I don't know."

They pulled into the hospital emergency lot twenty minutes later. The desk nurse took quick, basic information, then sent them upstairs.

"Timothy Gallagher." Grant spoke his son's name in a firm, tight voice. "They just brought him in."

"We're getting him settled." The calm night nurse took them into a nearby waiting area, overlooking the city lights. "Give us a little time to stabilize him."

Stabilize him. The phrase put a choke hold on Emily's heart. "His doctor just arrived, and she'll be able to fill you in shortly." She pointed to a coffee system and a food cupboard. "Help yourself to anything, and be assured that Timmy is in good hands right now."

Grant didn't reply, and when Emily looked up, she realized he couldn't reply. Harsh emotion marked his gaze, his face. His throat convulsed and he blinked hard, twice. She reached out and took his hand. "Thank you. We'll be right here, waiting for the doctor."

Minutes ticked by like hours. Christa texted Grant about the wedding as the sun broke along the eastern horizon, and Grant scrubbed a hand to his face. "The wedding. How can I think about the wedding at a time like this? But how can I not think about the wedding?"

Emily took his phone and texted a quick message of reassurance to Christa, then handed the phone back. "The wedding's in good hands—everything's been checked and rechecked. That's why you hired us, Grant. We've got your back. Right now the only thing you need to worry about is Tim."

"And Dolly. What if she gets it? She's more prone to things than Tim."

"She's as tough as they come. Tougher than you give her credit for."

He scowled at the door, then faced her. "You're right about me overprotecting her."

"I know I am."

He flushed. "I never worry about Tim the same way. I fret about Dolly, about her limitations all the time, but I just kind of took Tim's health and well-being for granted. What kind of father does that?"

"The normal kind."

"What if I hadn't gotten up tonight? What if I hadn't gone to check on them? I don't, all the time. Usually, if all seems quiet I just go back to sleep. What if I'd done that, Emily, and lost him?"

She held his gaze. "I call those Holy Spirit nudges. Those instincts that come for no reason, out of the blue. I believe God uses the Holy

Spirit to nudge our conscience to do good. To choose well."

"God makes house calls?" He sounded cryptic, but he was stressed so she let it ride.

"He does *every* kind of call. He promised to be wherever two or more are gathered in his name."

"Em." He stared out, over the city, and exhaled slowly. "I wish I had your faith. Your beliefs. I—" He stopped talking and turned quickly when the doctor strode in.

"How is he? Can I see him?"

The doctor motioned to a chair. Grant shook his head. "No, I don't need to sit. Just tell me, straight out. Is he going to be okay?"

"Well, I'll sit then, because it's going to be a long day." The doctor sank into a chair. Grant didn't look any too happy, but he followed her lead. Emily did, too, and folded her hands in silent prayer.

"He's got pneumonia."

"Pneumonia?" Grant shook his head. "How can he? He hasn't been sick. He had sniffles for a day or two, but nothing that would give you pneumonia."

"Whooping cough does."

"He's got whooping cough?" Emily sat forward. "I've been watching him for the past several days, Doctor, and he hasn't really been coughing."

"Not everyone gets the textbook cough."

"He's been vaccinated." Grant gripped the arms of the chair. "How could he come in contact with someone with whooping cough?"

"It's highly contagious and we're seeing more cases even with the vaccine. In Tim's case I'm going to keep him here and monitor him until the antibiotic takes hold and gives him the upper hand. But I want to put Dolly on a course of antibiotics starting immediately. We don't want this bacteria lurking in her system, so we're taking a proactive approach."

"Of course. I just don't see how he could get something like this."

"Exposure to someone harboring the bacteria. And everyone Tim has been around this week has been exposed."

"I've taken them all over this week, Doctor," Emily told her. "In and out of town, visiting people. Did I cause a new pandemic?"

The doctor laughed. "No, but we will get the word out. Babies are especially susceptible, as are children with health issues. No blame to spread here—these things happen. I'll write you a prescription, and yes you can stay right here with Tim. We'll probably keep him here for forty-eight hours or until he turns the corner and I'm confident about his prognosis. Is there someone who can watch Dolly?"

"My sister and I will."

"Good. I'm going to send a prescription over to the pharmacy in Grace Haven, the one I usually use for you, Grant. That hasn't changed, has it?"

"No, the Grace Haven Pharmacy is fine."

"And they should have it in stock, so you can pick it up later this morning. If not, I'll forward it to another drugstore. I want Dolly fighting this sooner rather than later."

"I'll call my sister to pick it up," offered Emily. "She's right there in town."

"All right." The doctor stood. "I'm going to take you in. He looks funny right now because we've medicated him and we're giving him IV fluids. We've got oxygen on him just to help ease his struggle. You're not going to freak out on me, are you, Grant?"

He shook his head, but the sadness in his gaze broke Emily's heart. "I'll be fine."

"Okay. Let's go."

Chapter Twelve

Grant's heart seized and his breathing went tight when he saw Tim hooked up to various tubes and machines. His vibrant, sturdy, smart little boy looked suddenly helpless.

His stomach knotted.

His hands formed fists.

Tears smarted his eyes, but he needed to be strong for Tim. Strong for Dolly. He brushed the back of his hand against his face and leaned over the high-sided bed. "Hey, buddy. Daddy's here. I'll be here with you all day, okay? I love you, Timmers." He leaned in and kissed his son, choking back emotion.

He worried about Dolly constantly. He fretted nonstop, he overprotected her, and he kind of just expected Tim to be okay. And now he wasn't. Guilt mushroomed inside him.

"He'll sleep for a while." The doctor kept

her voice soft. "The nurses are monitoring his breathing, his oxygen and his fluids. We started with an IV antibiotic and we'll go to an oral once he's better."

"But he's going to be all right? He'll recover?"

The doctor put a hand on Grant's arm. "He should be fine, but there is a slight mortality rate. Let us do our jobs while you guys continue to pray for him."

Pray for him.

Grant swallowed hard. He hadn't prayed in a long time. Not since he got down on his knees as a little boy, begging God to bring his daddy back.

It never happened, and he decided right then that God didn't exist because if he did, could he ignore a child's plea like that? And if he could, then Grant wanted nothing to do with him.

Prayer hadn't been part of his college life, or his work life or his married life. In Grant's opinion it was old-school nonsense, a simplistic way to handle complex issues.

Now it was life and death, his child, his beloved son. He bowed his head.

What should he say? How should he start? And why would God cast favor on a stubborn nonbeliever like Grant?

Emily prayed softly and sweetly, murmuring

words of supplication, asking God to bless Tim, to bless Dolly, to bless Grant.

God owed him nothing. Grant knew that. But if he could see his way clear to heal Tim and keep Dolly from getting sick, Grant would be forever in his debt.

Seven hours and no change.

Tim's pallor didn't make Emily nervous: it downright scared her. Pale, waxy skin. Washed-out lips. Faded fingernails.

The doctor had been in twice, and the last time she'd been accompanied by an infectious disease control specialist. They conferred in soft tones, backfilling the room with murmured words behind the hums and clicks of machines.

And then they left, leaving Grant and her wondering.

A young woman came to the door. "I've got a coffee cart here. Can I make you something special?"

"No, I—" Grant began, but Emily stood and moved across the room.

"Yes. Absolutely. I'd love a mocha latte, and straight coffee for my friend, here."

The young woman smiled, fixed their coffees then handed Emily a small tray of fresh bagels and cream cheese. "Just in case."

"Thank you." Emily whispered the words and

took the food over to the small side table near the window. She pulled back the curtain partway.

Bold winter sun brightened the room. The angled light got Grant's attention. He stood and stretched. Worry etched his face. "I'm sorry to mess up your day."

"You didn't." She handed him his coffee. "He did." She indicated the sick toddler with a smile. "But it's kind of special to have the chance to come and sit by his side and pray him through this."

"What if—"

She held up a firm hand. "We don't go to what-ifs. We go to whens. *When* Tim turns the corner, we take him home. *When* Tim is better, he'll tease and torture his sister again. *When* Tim feels good, he'll want ice cream. Get it?"

He smiled, and it was the first smile she'd seen all day, then he reached out and hugged her with one arm. "Got it." He rested his chin on top of her hair. "Thank you for being here. I couldn't have gotten through this without you."

"You're welcome." His arm, slung gently around her. Being tucked in, close to his side. The feel of his chest, rising and falling with each breath. Yes, even sharing his concern for this beautiful child, struggling to fight off illness. Emotion rose within her. Sweet emotion, tender thoughts of what could be, shoving No-el's lucrative offer out of contention.

He'd prayed with her today. It took a near-death experience, but he'd turned his son over to God, the Father Almighty, and for a stubborn, take-charge guy like Grant, begging was a huge step. Was this a real change or a God-of-convenience thing?

Who knew? But it was a move in the right direction.

Corinne tiptoed into the room just then. "Hey, guys. I have tonight off so I brought some necessities from home. New toothbrushes and toothpaste, some fruit, chocolate—" She arched a knowing brow in Emily's direction. "And a picture from Dolly." She held up a sheet of construction paper covered with scribbles. "Rory put this on an art board and gave her a box of toddler crayons. This handcrafted work of art is her gift to you. And I'm supposed to tell you that she's had her first dose of the antibiotic and will get her second dose right about now."

Grant looked relieved as he accepted the drawing. "Thank you. And thank Rory again for me, okay? You Gallaghers know how to step up to the plate."

"Well, we're baseball lovers." Corinne grinned as if that was a given.

"There is that." Grant's slight smile didn't

erase the concern in his eyes as he watched Tim for any sign of improvement. "But it's more than a good analogy. It's how you live." His mouth pressed tight. "I didn't realize how rare that was. I've spent so much time coasting through life, I never realized how important some things were."

Sympathy swelled within Emily. "We all make mistakes. And life hands us curveballs. Oops. Sorry. Baseball again."

He touched her cheek with his free hand, a gentle gesture. "It was stupid that it took me this long to see things more clearly. To understand better."

"I think we come to moments at different points in our lives," Corinne told him. "And what we make of those choices, those bends in the road, helps mold us. We can't change what's been, but we can be a blessing to what will be."

Tim moved just then. He wriggled on the bed. His face contorted, then he yawned, a big old normal, little-kid yawn. He blinked, peeked around then dozed back off, but for just a moment, he looked delightfully normal.

"Did you see that?"

Corinne laughed softly. "I think the meds are kicking in and we've got bacteria on the run."

"You think?"

She pointed to the tips of his fingers, now a healthier-looking pink. "Yup."

"Oh, man." Grant grabbed hold of his son's bed rails and breathed relief. "This has been a day for the record books. First, Serenity's call, saying she was in town and wanted to see me. Then having Tim get sick and rushing him into the hospital. I would be okay with never having to do this again."

"It's parenthood, Grant. Trust me." Corinne smiled down at the little one in the bed. "It will happen again."

Emily appreciated her advice, but she zeroed in on Grant's first statement. "You said Serenity is in town?"

Grant grimaced. "Someplace, yes. She wanted to see me, without the kids. I said no, of course."

"Why?" Foreboding took the place sympathy had held, because Emily was pretty sure she knew why.

"She walked out. She made choices. Why should I let her waltz back in when she feels like it? We've had no contact from her in two years. Not even a Christmas card. No." He shook his head. "She didn't need us. We don't need her."

And there it was, the quiet knell of confirmation.

Christ had talked about forgiveness.

Grant had none. He'd taken old hurts and

turned them into a life sentence. He casually examined both sides of the issues and chose stubborn anger each time. His firm jaw and squared shoulders said he meant business.

Well, so did she. And it didn't include a life full of drama, anger and angst.

"Hey, I see good news on the monitors." The doctor strode in, looking more cheerful than she had two hours before. "He's oxygenating better, and his pulse rate is coming back to normal. The meds are doing their job."

"He'll be okay?" The hope in Grant's voice reflected Emily's, but she put her heart in pause mode.

"It looks like we're on the road back," the doctor told him. "We'll continue treatment here until I'm sure, and then you'll have to be vigilant at home. This is a tough bacteria, and we can't get comfortable or let down our defenses. No taking him out, dragging him around, wearing him down, okay? He needs to be at home, quiet and cozy, all right?"

"We'll see to it," Grant promised.

"Good. I'll check back later." She left the room, humming, a much more cheerful sound than the earlier quiet of hushed voices.

Grant swung around and gave Emily a nice big hug. "Did you hear that? He's going to be okay!"

"I heard."

"Aren't you thrilled?" he asked, clearly pleased and relieved by the doctor's prognosis. "I thought you'd be doing a happy dance."

She looked up. Met his gaze. Held it. "His mother is in town."

Grant nodded. "Yes."

"And her little boy was rushed to a hospital in the middle of the night, and you never called her, Grant."

He stared at her. "She left. That was her choice, not ours."

"But she's his mother." She moved to the side of the bed and brushed back a lock of hair from Tim's forehead as she whispered her goodbye. "What if this had gone all wrong? What if Tim hadn't made it through the night? Then would it be all right for you to deny his mother the chance to see him one last time?"

His frown said she surprised him. Didn't he realize that every decision, large and small, had consequences? Or did he just not care? Either way, she needed to quietly walk away from this attraction. She breathed deep and took a firm step back. "I'm heading home with Corinne. We'll keep Dolly as long as we need to, so don't worry a thing about her. Keep in touch, okay? Let us know how he's doing." Decision made, she moved toward the door.

"Emily."

She didn't turn, didn't look back, didn't pause. She couldn't.

How could he do that? No matter what Serenity had done, no matter that his ego got crushed and his feelings hurt, knowing she was in town and not contacting her when Tim could have died—

Her heart clenched. Her breath caught. She couldn't talk, couldn't think about this now and maintain control in the vibrant-colored children's hospital, surrounded by strangers immersed in their own dramas.

Tim was doing better. Her heart sang with joy over that, but realizing that Grant chose anger over forgiveness wasn't just a red flag. It was a big bold stop sign.

Faith, forgiveness and trust were key factors in life.

She knew that change had to come from within Grant. She saw that clearly today. She followed Corinne to her car, climbed in and let the tears fall.

She still had a wedding to handle for him, a beautiful and well-planned celebration for Grant's sister. She'd do it well, with a pageant-worthy smile firmly in place.

And then she'd tiptoe out of the twins'—and Grant's—lives and never let anyone see the ache she held inside.

* * *

Grant watched Emily leave and knew it was a final straw.

Why would she think badly of him for not pulling Serenity in when Timmy got sick? It was coincidence, pure and simple, that had Serenity in the area now. Not love of family, and certainly not any regard for these wonderful children.

Anger simmered within him. Emily didn't understand. She'd never had anyone walk out on two babies. How could she judge him when she'd never walked a mile in his shoes?

He was tired. She was tired. Maybe this wouldn't seem so dire after they both got some sleep.

He texted her a late-afternoon picture of Timmy awake, eating a freeze pop.

Her reply was Dolly loves seeing Timmy! She sends her love!

He texted back, Can you keep Dolly overnight?

One word. One tiny word. Yayuh.

Her stretched-out version of yes made him smile while his heart ached. He dozed fitfully in the chair. Images of Timmy and Dolly kept him from falling into a deep sleep. He woke up early, rubbed sleep from his eyes and went into the bathroom to wash his face.

Solemn. Stern. Forbidding.

He stared into the mirror.

Was he always like this? So rigid, so sure he was right?

The mirror told him nothing, but his conscience wasn't as reticent. *You're foolishly stubborn in your personal life. That's no one's fault but your own. Why would a wonderful woman like Emily Gallagher be attracted to you? You're gruff and grumpy.*

"Fweeze pop, pwease? Daddy, Tim have a fweeze pop, pwease?"

Emotions rolled up inside him. Joy that Timmy was coming around, and frustration. Frustration at himself, at life, at people unwilling to do their best.

Serenity abandoned her family, just like his father had. Grant had done no such thing. He'd stayed the course. Therefore...

Therefore, what? No one gets a second chance in the McCarthy house? What a wretched way to live.

"Hey!" Timmy stood, waggling his arms, delighted to see Grant. "Timmy have fweeze pop, pwease?"

He looked down at his beloved son, and really looked this time.

Serenity's eyes smiled up at him from his boy's face. Serenity's smile, too.

No matter how angry he was, Emily had hit the nail on the head. He should have called her when Timmy went into crisis. It was the right thing to do.

When had he decided he had the right to command everything?

You wanted Serenity to come back begging forgiveness, seeing the error of her ways. And when she did come back, you didn't have the guts enough to see her. Why?

He didn't know, but he knew one thing. Two, actually. His boy needed a freeze pop, and he needed to man up and reach out to his ex-wife. No mother deserved to be left in the dark about life-and-death matters.

He got Tim a freeze pop and pulled out his cell phone.

Dead.

He groaned.

"You sad?" Tim reached up and touched Grant's face with sticky, chilled fingers. "Daddy sad?"

"Daddy's fine, honey. Just…aggravated."

"I sowwy." Timmy snuggled into him. They'd unhooked his IVs, and it was so good to see him awake, talking and smiling. His heartfelt words opened Grant's eyes further.

He'd been scared to death just twenty-four hours ago. Witnessing Tim's improvement, fear had been vanquished, but he'd taken a hard look in the mirror once Emily left. The urge to fix things was strong, but he had no phone.

Thwarted.

He rocked Tim, watched a couple of cartoons with him and read him some stories, and when the doctor signed Tim's release papers with stern warnings about keeping him home for a couple of weeks, Grant took it to heart. He had stored-up vacation time coming. He took it, determined to see his little guy through this, but when Emily refused to answer his calls, he knew he'd be doing it alone. And that reality cut deep.

She wanted—no, forget that, she deserved the kind of man who went the distance. A man of honor, yes, but more than that: a man of faith. Of strength. Of forgiveness.

Could he be that man? Was he ever that person?

No, he realized, and the truth of that shamed him.

But he could be that person. He should be that person. Once he got home and got Timmy settled, he picked up the phone and dialed Serenity's number. She answered tentatively, with good reason. She knew him well and had no reason to believe he'd softened his heart. He blew out a breath and waded in. "I've changed my mind about meeting with you. I, um…" He paused, then said, "I shouldn't have brushed you off, Serenity, and I'm sorry. Can we still meet?"

"Yes." She paused, too, then went on. "I'm back in Baltimore right now, but I'm coming your way the first of the month. Is the coffee-house on Route 96 a good spot?"

"Sure."

"Then six o'clock, on the fourth? I get in that afternoon."

"Six is fine."

"I'll see you then. And thank you, Grant."

He hauled in a deep, slow breath, still torn, but wanting to do the right thing, finally. "You're welcome."

Chapter Thirteen

Timmy's recovery had made it both hard and easy to avoid Grant over the holidays, Emily realized. Hard because she really wanted to be there, sharing this time with him and caring for Tim.

But having Grant at home made it easier for her to step away, because Grant would be watching the kids himself.

The change gave her time to make plans for a new life. The prospect of Manhattan lay before her, but was it really the life she wanted?

It was the life you planned. The goal you set, the dream you had. Years of schooling, years of experience. What's changed?

She had, she realized as she walked home from church the first Sunday of January.

Quiet snow lay fresh on the ground, lit by thin sun and bright blue sky. A fair number of village folks walked to church on Sundays, even midwinter.

"Emily, good morning!"

She waved hello to Mrs. Rucker and her aging father.

"Good to see you, Emily!" Hi and Bertie Engle waved from the door of the Grace Haven Diner, a regular stop for them after church.

"Emily, Tank is wondering if Mags will be free for a play date this week?"

Old Mrs. Reinhart peered at her from her stoop. Snow still covered her walk, so Emily grabbed the shovel leaning against the small porch and proceeded to clean the snow off the elderly woman's sidewalk. "I'll bring Mags over today, if that's all right. And when I do, I'll take care of that driveway for you, Mrs. Reinhart."

"Oh, Emily." Mrs. Reinhart clasped a hand to her chest. "Would you, really? My Thomas is feeling the arthritis mighty bad these days, and he's that worried about the driveway not being done."

"I'll grab Amy and Callan, and we'll get it done in no time," Emily promised. "I'll hurry home and change into some proper shoveling clothes. See you soon!" She set the shovel back against the porch and started home, but something the aged woman said stuck with her.

Thomas Reinhart had arthritis and couldn't work the shovel.

Emily loved clothing design and specialty looks and putting those looks together.

Caroline Mason had worried about closing her shop because her rheumatoid arthritis had gotten bad.

A lightbulb clicked on in her rusty brain. It lit up tiny corners of her consciousness as though laughing at her. She'd been fussing and fuming about what to do for the past two months, and God had set a possible answer in front of her weeks ago.

Buy Caroline's Bridal.

Was she crazy?

No. She was perfectly sane with a great head for fashion and a buyout account from Barrister's Department Stores and her ex-husband.

Could she stay here comfortably, with Grant around?

She'd have to, she realized as she hurried up the steps to her parents' house. In the end, it all came down to choices. His and hers.

Did she love him?

This time she did sigh as she let herself into the big house.

Yes. Yes, she did. And she loved those children. The thought of losing Timmy had grabbed her by the heart the way nothing else could. But loving someone didn't mean you should compromise your principles. Love, faith and forgiveness went hand in hand, and Emily refused to settle for anything less than God's best.

She called Corinne and Kimberly to have Callan and Amy meet her at the Reinharts' driveway, and then she placed a call to Caroline Mason. And when she finally hung up the phone fifteen minutes later, Emily Gallagher had just bought herself a bridal salon.

Grant pulled into the strip mall parking lot just south of the thruway entrance. He stared at the well-lit café, worked his jaw, then climbed out of the car. He crossed the snowy lot and climbed the two steps when a voice called his name. "Grant."

He turned.

Serenity approached him from a bland rental vehicle. He wasn't sure what he'd expected, but the plain midsize sedan hadn't entered the imaginary picture. "Serenity."

"Thank you for seeing me." She studied his face, his eyes, his jaw, as if memorizing him, then stepped back for him to open the door.

He did. He let her precede him, and when they got inside, she moved to a table far from the entrance. "Coffee?" he asked.

She took a moment, then nodded. "Yes, please. A mocha, actually. If that's all right?"

Such an ordinary thing, having coffee, as if there hadn't been years of anger and discord between them. This moving on stuff wasn't exactly easy.

He ordered hers, then his, and when the barista handed him the drinks, he brought them back to the table. He set them down, then took the seat opposite her. "Listen, I—"

"Grant, I—"

They both paused. Grant made a face. "Let me go first, because I need to apologize and I don't have a lot of practice, a fact which needs to change."

"Apologize?" She sat straighter. "Why?"

"For being an unforgiving, sanctimonious jerk who tried to keep you away from me and your children when you asked. And for not calling you when Timmy got sick in December."

"He got sick? Is he better? And how's Dolly?" She leaned forward. Her coat fell open. She gathered it back around her and shivered slightly.

"Are you that cold? We could ask them to turn up the heat."

She shook her head. "I get cold easy. It's no big deal."

It was a big deal because she didn't look comfortable. She looked worn and tired, now that he looked more closely. "You're sure?"

"Yes. So. Back to the kids. Is Tim doing better?"

"He is, but he had to stay low-key for a couple of weeks. He caught whooping cough somehow, and it turned into pneumonia."

"Grant, how frightening that must have been." She looked genuinely concerned.

"It was. I may have overreacted a little."

She smiled softly, and for a brief moment he was transported back a dozen years to the woman he fell in love with. "You? Who'd have thought?"

"Anyway, he was hospitalized and I should have called you and I didn't, and I'm sorry about that. Listen." He leaned forward to catch her gaze. "I know the whole parenting thing wasn't your gig. You made that clear." He raised his shoulders slightly. "But they're amazing and delightful and I love them. I love caring for them. And I'm sorry we stopped sharing the same dream somewhere along the way, and if one of them ever gets sick like that again, I'll call you and let you know. Okay?"

She didn't look up for a long time. She blinked, not once or twice, but three times, then dashed a hand across her face.

"You're crying." He grabbed a few napkins

from the table dispenser and handed them over. "I didn't mean to make you cry." Remorse hit him again. No matter what he did, he couldn't seem to manage the right steps with people lately. "Serenity, I—"

"No." She held up a hand, swiped the napkins to her cheeks, then faced him square. "You didn't make me cry. Well, not just you. Life's got a way of doing that on its own."

He frowned.

"I'm sick, Grant." She reached out and grasped both of his hands in hers. "All those newfangled ideas doctors are coming up with about how to treat cancer are going to miss me by a year or two." She squeezed his hands. "I'm dying."

He couldn't have heard her correctly. He stared, and when she gripped his hands tighter he finally found words. "You're kidding, right?"

"Nobody kids about cancer, Grant."

She was right.

"I found out a few months ago. It's ovarian, it's already spread and I'm opting out of treatment."

"You're what?" Surprise and concern claimed him. "You're not fighting?"

She let go of his hands and sipped her mocha. "I'm beyond fighting. I decided to savor these last few months fixing things that never should have been broken."

"That's why you came back to town."

She nodded slowly. "Cancer is a wake-up call. And I woke up realizing I'd become a selfish person, hung up on appearances. I didn't like that about myself." She ran her finger around the rim of the cup, thinking. "I decided I wanted to change what I can and I'd like to go home to God knowing you don't hate me."

Him, again. Not the kids. He frowned. "I don't hate you. And I'm moving beyond the anger at last because it's a stupid waste of energy. But I don't get it, Serenity." He leaned forward when she looked up.

"Get what?"

"You don't want to see the kids? Be with them? Especially when you have so little time?" It hurt him to say those words. A physical ache formed inside him, like a yawning hole.

"They won't remember me." She spoke softly. "I've been gone, they don't know me, they'll never have the chance to know me. Why confuse them at this point? That seems like a grossly unfair thing to do to little children, Grant."

He reached out. Took her hands. Tears slipped down her cheeks, to the table below. "They won't always be small. And when they get bigger and ask about their mother, I'd love to have some pictures of you with them to show them. Stay here awhile, Serenity. If money's tight, I'll cover the cost."

She looked embarrassed, so he knew money had become an issue.

"I want us to part as friends." He leaned closer to see her downturned face. "And I want our children to have a chance to know the wonderful woman who gave birth to them."

He let go of her hands and waited. She pulled some more napkins from the dispenser and swiped her cheeks, her eyes. "Are you sure?"

"Positive."

"You've changed, Grant."

He winced on purpose. "I had to change. I was being a jerk about a lot of things, and then…"

"Then?"

He took a long, slow draw on his coffee. "Then God started opening doors and windows, but I was typically stupid and ran around closing them all. You know that expression, can't see the forest for the trees?"

"All too well."

"Well, me, too. I was so busy thinking I had all the answers, I never paused to examine the questions. Now I do."

"I'm glad."

"Me, too. Are you hungry, Serenity?"

She made a face. "Not much appetite."

"Can we go get your stuff? Move you to the inn at Grace Haven?"

"My mom's with me."

"We'll move you both over, then. I'm glad she's here."

"She'd like to see the kids now and again, Grant." She lifted one shoulder as if hedging her request. "When I'm gone."

Her words pierced his heart. How foolish they'd been to waste precious time, as if life was a given, not a treasured gift. "Absolutely."

She wavered when she stood. He rounded the table and took her arm. When they got outside, her mother approached from the sedan. "Jacqueline." He reached out and grasped her hand with his free one. "You should have come in."

She took her daughter's arm and gazed up at him with heartbroken eyes. "She needed to see you alone, Grant. How are the children? Are they well?"

"They are, Mom." Serenity sounded relieved. "We'll get to see them. Tomorrow?" Serenity faced Grant.

"Tomorrow, yes." Sudden concern broadsided him. "What if you catch something from them?"

She held his gaze. "A risk worth taking."

He agreed wholeheartedly. "Jacqueline, I'm

going to move you two to the inn in town. Do you remember where that is?"

"Yes."

"Do you need help getting your things?"

She shook her head. "We traveled light on purpose. I'll drive back to the hotel and gather everything. It won't take long."

"And I'll call the inn and make sure there's room, but this time of year that shouldn't be a problem." He made the call, booked the room and hung up the phone. "Come right over to the house in the morning, okay? Don't waste time."

Serenity reached out and hugged him.

His heart ached and expanded. "I'm glad you came to meet me."

"Me, too."

He helped her into the car. Now that she'd told him, the difference was remarkable. She looked more relaxed, but drawn. Hollowed eyes, a lax jaw, but in her gaze he glimpsed a commitment he hadn't seen in a lot of years. He waved them off, climbed into his SUV and drove back home, remonstrating himself.

What if he hadn't had a change of heart? What if Emily hadn't called him on his behavior? What if he'd gone on, never letting Serenity see her children? How would he have atoned for a grievous mistake like that?

God's timing. Instead of ignoring it, he'd embraced it, all because Emily Gallagher called him out and walked away.

He came into the house, drained. Tillie and Percy had just settled the kids into bed. Quiet reigned.

"They were good as gold." Tillie tried to whisper, but Tillie's bad hearing made even her soft voice loud. "Percy grabbed the mail from the box—it's there on the counter. You got a letter from Christa and you need milk."

He'd forgotten to stop for milk while digesting Serenity's news. "I'll get it on the way home tomorrow."

"And the kids are doing okay with the new day care lady?"

He nodded. "She's very nice, and Mary should be back in four weeks. But yes, they both like her."

"Good!" Uncle Percy had gone out to warm up their car. Tillie hugged him. "A busy month with the wedding and all, and then back to normal." She bustled out the door and pulled it snug behind her.

Normal.

Emily gone.

Serenity's tragic news.

And in his hand he held a letter from his beloved sister. He stared at the letter, almost unwilling to open it. Their last phone conversation had been a disaster. Would the letter chew him out?

Probably, and deservedly so.

He sank into the broad recliner and didn't turn on the weeknight football game like he normally would. He held the letter in his hand, and then did something Grant McCarthy hadn't done on his own in decades.

He prayed. He prayed for guidance, discernment and patience, and when he slit open the envelope and withdrew Christa's note, he was glad he did.

Dear Grant,
First, I love you. You have been more than just a big brother to me. You've been my best friend. My confidant. So when you read this, I want you to understand I'm not trying to hurt you. A soldier learns early that the truth sets us free, and that honor and honesty go hand in hand. And that's the crux of this letter.

Our father didn't coldly abandon us. He tried to see us many times. When I was in Colorado, he showed me the letters to Mom and her replies.

He had no money. He was in treatment for post-traumatic stress disorder. He'd made mistakes, then worked really hard to clean himself up and get his head on straight. (His words.)

She wouldn't see him. She wouldn't let him see us. And she got a restraining order against him when he came to town.

Grant, I'm not making excuses for him. I don't minimize your pain at being thrust into a caretaker role as a child. But I don't want to go on bearing a grudge.

Whatever you decide is fine with me, really it is. But I needed you to see the truth of the matter.

Our mother was a great woman in many ways, but she had a hard side. It makes me sad that for all of her dedication to church and faith, she never found it in her heart to forgive Dad. I am determined to make sure I don't make the same mistake.

With great love,
Christa

Grant sat back in the chair and studied the note.

The truth of her words hit him square.

He knew his mother. He understood the gravity of her stubbornness. Had he let the facade of her Christianity color her too sweetly?

He sighed, because he knew he had. And hadn't he just recognized similar qualities in himself?

Yes.

He read the letter again, and somewhere deep inside a flicker of hope sparked into life.

His father hadn't simply walked out on them. He'd tried to make contact.

All these years he'd lived in the shadow of a lie, and his mother allowed them to believe it. She'd encouraged them to believe it. She'd let anger turn her to deceit, at the expense of her children's relationship with Joe McCarthy.

He gripped the letter hard, thinking, and then he got up. He moved to the computer and typed his father's name into the search engine. When Joe McCarthy's name came up outside Denver, Grant reached out and picked up the phone.

His sister was right. Life was too short to live it under a cloud of anger and resentment. He dialed his father's number, and when Joe's voice said hello, over thirty years of shadowed sorrow began to melt away. "Dad? It's me. Grant. How are you?"

"Grant."

There was no missing the tight emotion in his father's voice, the slightly ragged breath that came afterward. "It's really you? Oh my gosh, son, how are you? I can't believe this, I can't—"

A short gasp for air followed, as if Joe couldn't believe his ears.

Grant knew how hard it was to talk, because he felt exactly the same way. The voice... Joe's inflection...so similar to his. "I've missed you, Dad. So much."

He was pretty sure that big, strong Joe McCarthy was emotional on the other end of the phone. He knew he was. Over thirty years gone. Wasted in anger. Cloaked in resentment.

"I miss you, too. I can't even say how much, son."

The thought of his mother, purposely keeping them apart, struck him deep, but then another image bloomed. Sweeter. Even stronger.

Seventy times seven. That's how often you should forgive those who hurt you.

Grant took a deep breath. He might not have been a churchgoer for a long time, but he remembered that teaching from childhood and he wasn't about to repeat his mistakes. He was not going to spend the next decades resenting or hating his mother.

He was going to leave the past where it belonged, in the past, and move toward a new future. "Dad, I don't know if this is possible, but Christa's getting married next week. Would it be possible for you to come? And your family, of course." It sounded and felt weird to say that, but almost good, too. "I've got enough money in the wedding fund to cover the tickets."

"We'd love to come," Joe replied. "And I appreciate the offer, but we can foot the tickets on this end. Grant." A sigh came through the phone, filled with relief. "I can't wait to see you."

"You can meet your grandchildren."

"Best news ever, when Christa told me that," Joe declared. "If you give me your email, I'll send you our flight information as soon as I book them."

Grant gave him the address. Dolly squawked in her room, and Grant stood up. "Dad, one of the kids is waking up, I've got to go. I'll see you next week, okay?"

He'd have to be really hard of hearing not to hear the joy in his father's voice. "Yes, it's very okay."

He walked to Dolly's room and peeked in. She lay curled back up, sound asleep.

He tiptoed away, back to the great room, then unlocked the sliding glass door and stepped outside. Cold, crisp air greeted him. The house blocked the west wind, but swirling snow danced and drifted around the corners, forming new mounds.

He stared up, into the sky, clear and bright and huge. He'd moved forward today, in ways he'd never have imagined just a few weeks ago, and it felt good. So good.

But losing Emily shadowed the accomplishment. Was this another side of selfishness, this longing for her to stay right here, in Grace Haven, with him?

Or was it the simple and beautiful love of a man for a woman?

The latter, he decided as the cold bit his cheeks. In the end, the decision would be hers. But in the meantime, he wanted to give her every possible reason he could to stay.

Chapter Fourteen

Emily and Kimberly were busily putting together a flowchart of spring events and summer weddings when their mother called the next day. Emily clicked the button and warned, "You're on speaker, Mom, and Kimberly's here so don't say anything mean about her, okay?"

"I can't yell at you on speaker, Emily." Kate sounded perturbed, but not really angry. "Take me off speaker where I can ream you out in private."

"It's more fun this way, Mom!" Kimberly exchanged an amused look with Emily. "I love it when she's the one in trouble. Go for it!" To Emily she whispered, "Do you have any idea what she's talking about? What have you done?"

"I got nothin'," Emily whispered back. Then she spoke in a louder voice. "It can't be too bad,

Mom, because I've been too busy to have done too much wrong. Trust me on that."

"Noel Barrister contacted us."

Emily stared at the desk phone, mouth open. "He what?"

"Uh-oh." Kimberly made a face of mock horror. "This sounds good."

"He told us he made you a very lucrative offer, with employment guarantees, and a New York office. He reminded us that this is a chance-of-a-lifetime deal and that we are selfishly holding you back from living your dream. Emily, why didn't you tell us? You know we'd never do that. All your father and I have ever wanted was for our girls to be wonderful women, full of life and love, living your dreams. If this is what you want, you should do it, honey. Although the thought of you working for the Barristers again doesn't exactly top my list," she added in a more dour tone. "But if this is your dream—"

"Mom." Emily sighed out loud on purpose to interrupt her mother. It worked. "First, I love you."

"Emily Rose, I—"

"My turn," she interrupted smoothly. "Let me finish. I love you guys to pieces, and while I'm actually learning to enjoy my job here with Kimberly and I've gotten better at this whole event-planning thing, I'm not great at it like she is, so I'm turning in my full-time notice as of six o'clock next Tuesday."

"You're what?" The look of surprise on Kimberly's face was worth the momentary shock value. "You're taking his job offer? Seriously?"

"But Emily, he just called and said—"

"Hang on, both of you." Emily held up a hand to stave off Kimberly's reaction just as Rory came into the room. "I'm not taking Noel's offer. I'm not going anywhere. I'm staying right here in Grace Haven and if Kimberly needs or wants help, I'll be available nearby because…" She flashed her sisters a delighted grin. "I'm buying Caroline's Bridal. We do the closing on Tuesday, and I am absolutely delighted to be staying in town."

"You're buying Caroline's? For real?" Kimberly grabbed her shoulders, then hugged her, hard. "I knew she was having health issues, and I was hoping someone would step in because losing the only bridal shop in town would be terrible! Oh, Em!" Kimberly hugged her again, as if she just couldn't stop. "This is perfect. We'll be just up the road from each other, and we can give each other backup as needed."

"My thoughts exactly," Emily agreed happily. "And then there's Rory." She sent a teasing look to her younger sister.

"Who has no plans to do anything bridal,

ever, so you two just go on with your own little Gallagher bridal dynasty and I'll cheer from the sidelines."

Kate laughed through the phone. "Emily, I'm over-the-moon delighted that you decided to do this. It's right up your alley! And knowing the two of you can work together as needed—"

"A welcome change, right?" Emily met Kimberly's gaze, and they both laughed.

"And I'm sure Grant is thrilled."

Kimberly's eyes went wide. The room grew quiet. Emily hadn't brought up Grant's name since walking away from him a few weeks before. Kimberly and Rory had both respected her silence, with regular gifts of chocolate. But now—

Kimberly waded in to save her. "Well, why wouldn't he be? With his sister's wedding coming up this week, life's been crazy, but we're going to celebrate Emily's new business as soon as Christa's wedding is over."

"Perfect timing!" declared Kate. "Girls, I've got to run—Dad's due back from his treatment any minute. He's looking worn, but the treatment appears to be working. Keep praying, okay?"

"Haven't stopped, Mom, and no worries. Everything's fine here."

"I'm sure it is, dears. If you gals can handle

the Yorkos family, you can handle anything. Goodbye! I love you!"

They disconnected the call. Almost on cue, Allison buzzed them from the first floor. "Stella Yorkos is here to see you, Emily. And I have a delivery down here you need to sign for."

Stella and Kimberly in the same venue meant Kimberly was about to learn the details of the Worst Bridal Shower Ever, but Emily realized it couldn't be helped. She led the way downstairs, dreading the confrontation as she prepared herself mentally. Rory slipped out the back door to go home as Emily started toward Stella.

Allison motioned her toward the delivery person first. "Signature here, please."

"It has to be me?" Emily asked out loud, surprised. Allison usually signed for anything as needed, but when she drew close, she saw the framed, unwrapped package on Allison's desk and caught her breath. "Oh good heavens, can you possibly even stand the cuteness?" She jotted her initials into the signature box and lifted the picture as the delivery man strode out through the back door. In her hands she held a wonderful picture of Dolly and Timmers, all dressed up, looking like a pair of absolutely adorable country kids. A small card was attached. Emily lifted the flap while Kimberly greeted Stella behind her. "Miss you, Em. We *all* miss you. With love, Grant."

Her heart wound up, then down.

She missed them, too. She missed Grant's gentle gaze, his strength, his warmth, the ingrained dedication of a good man. But without faith and a forgiving heart—

She blinked back emotion, winced when she met Allison's gaze and took a step back. Stella was waiting, and she didn't want to be rude or put off reckoning any longer. She turned and was surprised, no, make that *struck dumb* to see Stella smiling. As Emily approached, Stella came toward her.

And then Stella hugged her.

Numb with surprise, she looked at Kimberly over Stella's shoulder and arched a brow in question.

Kimberly shrugged, equally at a loss.

Stella ended the quick embrace, stepped back and met her gaze. "I came to apologize for my behavior and to thank you for standing by me at that train wreck of a shower."

Kimberly looked interested now. Really interested.

"I don't know what came over me, or why I let my mother's influence push so many buttons, but seeing her in action that day, seeing how many people she hurt on purpose, was like looking in a mirror. And I didn't like what I saw.

"Your sister—" she turned back toward Kimberly "—put up with my hysterics like a pro. She had no reason to be nice to me, but she was, and in the midst of utter craziness, Emily was the calm in her storm. Thank you, Emily." She redirected her attention toward Emily. "Scott and I have it all worked out with his family, and they're still coming to the wedding. And Katelyn is still my flower girl, with the right kind of dress this time. Now that we're into the new year, I wanted to personally express my gratitude. You went above and beyond, and I'll never forget it. And I'll let everyone know just how amazingly wonderful Kate & Company is."

Emily couldn't believe her ears.

She'd expected a full reaming for whatever reason. Instead Stella's apology rang sweet and true. "It was a rough situation, but it's all worked out." She took Stella's hand. "Marriage is tough enough without the family drama thrown in."

"True." Stella took a step toward the door. "If there's anything we need to work out last-minute for my wedding, just call or text me. I'm going at this like I should have the whole time. Calm, well, mostly." She lifted one shoulder. "And happy. Like it should be."

She walked out and Kimberly turned to face

Emily. "'Train wreck of a shower'?" she quoted. She thrust a brow of interest up.

Emily winced. "A stunning debacle of the highest degree, but all's well that ends well, right?"

Kimberly burst out laughing. "Yes. In the end, that's what matters. Were you going to tell me?"

"Not in this lifetime."

Kimberly's expression indicated she understood that choice. She crossed to the desk and eyed the photograph of Grant's kids. "These two are beyond cute."

"I know."

"And yet?"

She looked at Kimberly and Allison and wished she could give them a different answer. "I found out how difficult marriage can be through experience. Falling in love isn't the hard part."

Allison nodded in understanding.

"Staying in love is the test, and if I ever get married again, I want a husband who walks to church with me. With our kids. Who forgives, even if he can't forget. Faith and a forgiving nature are the cornerstones of our parents' marriage. I don't want to settle for less than that, ever again. So that's how it goes." She studied the window and The Square beyond, the snow-dusted benches and snow-covered grass. "When my life fell apart, the last thing I wanted was to come back to Grace Haven." She motioned toward the quaint winter town outside their windows. "But I'm glad I did. I love it here. And I want to stay."

"Well, you have no idea how happy you've made me, because I'll be needing some time off come summer."

Emily turned, met Kimberly's gaze and understood immediately. "You're pregnant?" She didn't mean to screech, but she kind of accidentally did.

Kimberly put a finger to her lips as Allison hugged her.

"It's early, and we're keeping it hush until we're further along, but the fact that you're staying here makes this so much easier to plan."

Emily hugged her, too. "I'm absolutely crazy happy for you."

"Us, too. It didn't make sense to wait at my age. But we were a little surprised that it happened this quickly."

"'God is good,'" Emily quoted softly.

Kimberly finished the popular theme. "'All the time.'" She moved back to the planning board and tapped a finger against it. "And now, dear sister? Back to work."

"Absolutely." She picked up the photo Grant had sent and went back upstairs, determined.

She was excited for Kimberly and Drew. The thought of a new baby made her happy. She had to work to push aside thoughts of Grant and those two children. Their beautiful smiles, their funny antics, their endearing hugs.

She had fallen head over heels for Grant McCarthy. So much of who he was appealed to her. Strong, hardworking, tender, funny and focused.

She appreciated those down-to-earth qualities, but she'd taken faith and trust casually once. Big mistake. And it was a judgment error she never intended to make again, but each time she looked at the picture of those two kids, her heart ached a little bit more.

Marvelous kitchen scents accosted her when she walked into her parents' home that evening. Rory was in the kitchen, and the combination of smells meant her cooking skills were improving. She stabbed a spatula toward the table. "A package came for you."

"Another one?" Emily peeled off her gloves, scarf and coat and slung them on the back of a chair. She pulled open the cardboard zip tab, and inside was another picture for her. This one was of Grant and the kids. He was on the floor, playing with them, and the three of them looked delightfully happy.

A note slipped out and fluttered to the tabletop. Emily picked it up. The words made her heart go hard and soft all at once. "Something's missing from this picture, Em. I think it's you. With love, Grant."

Unfair tactics.

That's what he was employing right now, and days before she'd see him at Christa's wedding.

A text message came through about an hour later. Christa and Spencer have arrived. Need to check last-minute details of wedding. And possibly just need to see you. What time is good?

There wasn't a good time, but he was a client and she couldn't say no. Should she ask Kimberly to step in?

She texted back, Tonight at eight or tomorrow, midday.

Tonight. Can you come here?

She shouldn't because facing Grant on home turf made her wish she could be on his home turf more often, but she knew it was tough to have someone come in and watch the kids. Yes.

Perfect. See you then. Drive safe.

Nothing crazy personal like the pictures intimated, and in a way, that was better. Then why did she feel disappointed?

She helped Rory straighten up the kitchen,

tucked her purse and tablet into the car and pulled into Grant's driveway just before eight. The garage door rolled up before she got out of the car, and there he was, waiting for her.

Her heart danced.

Did his?

Her breath caught, but she was determined to blame that on the sharp west wind. And when he stood there, rock solid, so she'd have to either approach him or go through him, she drew close. "I'm here."

His eyes searched hers in the glow of the garage lights, and then he touched his two big, strong hands to her shoulders and smiled. "I'm glad. Christa and Spencer are waiting, and I've just put the kids to bed."

All business, then. No sticky fingers to wipe, no spills to clean up. Four adults, talking about a wedding. She could do this.

"Christa. Spencer." She extended her hand to each of them in turn once she got inside. "So nice to see you both, and Christa, Caroline told me how well the dress fitting went. Everything's in order, and I've got a checklist here." She brought up a page on the tablet and let them scroll through the list. "The only thing I wasn't sure of was your time frame, Grant." She stayed almost calm as she met his gaze, as if she didn't want to close the two feet between them and declare her feelings. "Are you bringing Dolly and Timmy home at some point when they get tired, and if so, are you able to return? I wanted to make sure with the DJ that you're included in all of the special events that mark a wedding day."

"The current plan is to have their mother and grandmother pick them up around six forty-five. They're going to bring them back here and watch them for the rest of the evening."

He'd made contact with Serenity.

She held his gaze, but didn't try to hide her smile of approval. "That's good to hear."

He smiled at her, as if her approval meant something to him, but then his face went sober. He leaned forward slightly. "She's sick, Emily."

Emily glanced at Spencer and Christa. The sorrow in Christa's expression reflected Grant's.

"It's cancer," Grant continued, "and she doesn't have a whole lot of time left. She and her mom are staying here in town so she can see the kids as often as possible."

"Grant." She reached out a hand and gripped his. "I'm so sorry."

"Me, too." He grimaced and ran his other hand through his hair. "But I'm glad you gave me a wake-up call, Em. That's what pushed me to contact her, and you were right. Living in anger isn't good for anyone. Because Serenity and Jacqueline will have the kids for the evening, anything you schedule with the DJ works for me."

"I'll take care of it." They noted a few more things, then she stood. "That's it, guys. Everything's in place. We're good to go."

"Thank you." Christa clasped her hand in both of hers. "Spencer and I are so grateful for your help, for guiding Grant through all of this. You've made everything seem so easy, and so right."

"She's got a gift."

Grant said the words casually, but when he reached out to help her get her coat in place, his hand brushed her cheek. And when she'd slipped her arm into the sleeve he stood right there, his hands on her shoulders, and then he repeated himself, softly. "A beautiful gift."

He stepped back then and swung the door wide. She walked through, wishing he'd walk out with her. Wishing for time, for words, for—

"I'll see you Saturday, Em."

She waved and fought the rise of disappointment. She was being silly. She'd walked away from him because he couldn't or wouldn't forgive. Now that he'd made a sincere effort, she should be happy for him. She was, but the sense of longing refused to fade. She backed down the driveway, sobered by his news about the twins' mother, but glad he'd stepped forward to resolve things. That was a major step in the right direction, and she was downright proud of him for doing it.

Chapter Fifteen

In his years as highway superintendent, Grant had handled blizzards, nor'easters, squalls, floods and two road collapses, but none of that compared to the past few days of nonstop organizing. With Christa's wedding just over three hours away, he was at the airport in a snowstorm to pick up the best wedding gift of all—Joe McCarthy and the rest of their Colorado family.

He hoped he'd done the right thing. It felt right, and Grant hadn't felt this way for a long while.

And when his father, stepmother and two siblings came through the door, Grant's chest went tight.

His father. Joe McCarthy.

Thin memories came back to him, of a big, tall man and a laughing little boy.

Grant moved forward. He stopped, awkward, wondering what he should say, then finally stuck out his hand and said, "Dad?"

Joe's eyes watered above a grin that matched Grant's. "Grant. It is so very good to see you, son."

He hugged Grant then, hugged him hard, as if he never wanted to let him go.

Grant's eyes smarted.

He remembered this hug, the feel of it. The feel of his father, embracing him.

"I've missed you, Dad." He didn't know he'd say those words. They tumbled out as if he was a kid, yearning for his father's time, his embrace, and maybe that's exactly what he was in this moment. A big, overgrown kid, finally in the arms of his father.

"Me, too." Joe hugged him tight, then kept an arm around him as he turned. "My wife, Linda."

"Ma'am." Grant gave her a hug and wasn't surprised to see her eyes water as she glanced from Joe to him and back again. "And this must be Maggie and Michael."

"Maggie's in her senior year at Colorado State and Mike's a sophomore at Oregon."

"And you're a runner, Mike?"

His younger brother nodded. "Middle distance. Oregon's a great place for runners."

"An excellent place," Grant agreed. "And Maggie, you're majoring in education?"

"A teacher, like Mom." She smiled at her mother, then turned a more shy version his way. "It's so good to meet you, finally. I hate family drama, and I love happily-ever-afters."

"She's our romantic," added Linda, smiling.

Joe chimed in. "I expect we better pick up our bags and get going. Will the snow hold us up?"

Grant cringed. "Well, we're getting lake-effect snow off Lake Ontario and Lake Erie, on top of the general storm that hit about an hour ago. We'll soon find out."

The SUV crawled across the expressway. Minutes ticked by far too quickly, erasing the opportunity to stop by the hotel and get changed into wedding clothes. Even with four-wheel drive, Grant couldn't get his SUV around the other vehicles bogged down in the snow.

He was running out of time. He made a quick call to Reverend Gallagher and explained the situation. Steve assured him that Joe's family could get ready at the abbey once they arrived. That was good news, but as Grant approached the thruway exit finally, the line of stuck cars proved insurmountable. If they didn't get these cars moved, and the exit cleared, a major thruway backup was about to occur.

"Dad? You got boots on?"

"I do."

"How about you, Mike?"

"Tall sneakers, just as good. I'm in."

Grant undid his seat belt. "Let's do this." The three men climbed out of the SUV. Grant put in a call to his department, explaining the growing problems at the thruway entrance and exit. He'd dispatched his plow operators hours earlier, and Jeannie was running things from the office, but the wet, heavy snow was winning the race against time.

He'd faced this before, and he'd lost a few of these snow-squall battles, but today he had to win. Today, the snow had to succumb to his timeline, because today his sister was getting married and her whole family was going to be there to celebrate. No stupid snowstorm was going to mess with his plans.

Grant pulled out the short shovel he kept tucked in the back of the SUV. Two other drivers had shovels in their stalled cars. Another driver, an elderly woman, offered them a short broom. They commandeered two shovels from the appreciative tollbooth attendant and got to work with other stuck-in-the-snow drivers.

Thirty minutes later, the exit was cleared of cars, and a plow truck was standing by, ready to open and salt the road. They climbed back into the car, tired and happy, with wet feet and pants.

"We don't look like wedding guests." Mike brushed snow from his hair onto Maggie. She laughed and tossed him a bib from the backseat. "I expect this is Timmy's because it says 'Almost as cute as my dad.' You can use it to dry your hair, Mikey."

Grant drove the SUV up to the main road, ruing the time lost. In good weather, the drive from here to the Abbey was about thirty-five minutes. With today's weather conditions, it was going to take them much longer.

As he was about to make the right turn toward town and the lake that sat beyond the town, one of his snow plows rumbled through the intersection. The driver paused, gave Grant a thumbs-up and then proceeded to plow the road literally in front of them.

"Now there's an escort for you!" Joe clapped Grant on the back. "Did you ask them to do that?"

He'd have never asked, but Jeannie must have figured out the problem and launched a solution. He shook his head, but smiled. "We've got good people here in Grace Haven."

"I'll say. At this rate, we should have just enough time to get inside, get changed and get into the chapel."

"Christa will cry," Grant warned them. "She has no idea you're coming, so expect waterworks."

Linda sat forward and touched Grant's arm. "You're a good man, Grant."

He shrugged, because he knew the truth. He'd been a jerk, plain and simple. He didn't deserve her kindness or her praise.

"And I'm sure I'm embarrassing you right now, but I wanted to tell you this." He gave her a quick glance in the rearview mirror. She met his gaze and spoke with warm conviction. "I'm sorry about what's gone on before. It left a lot of hurt feelings and lost time, but in spite of the rights and wrongs, your mother did a good job with you and your sister. Grown-up drama aside, she put her heart and soul into raising you both up right, and I hope we can all appreciate that."

Her words touched Grant in a special way.

It would be easy for Linda to hate his mother for the decades of hurt she caused Joe. Her gentle example set a loving tone of forgive and forget. It had taken him a long time to see the worth in that, and now the examples seemed to shine all around him.

Was that coincidence? Or God? And not the zealous, rigid way of God his mother espoused, but the soft, gracious faith he saw in Emily. In Linda. In Christa and his father.

He pulled into the far side of the Abbey at 2:40. Someone had plowed the service drive to the back door of the living quarters. Inside, the reverend's daughter showed everyone to a room in the retreat center, where they'd have plenty of space to get changed. He called home quickly as he changed into his own suit of clothes. The intense snow had forced a change in plans. Instead of coming to the wedding, Timmy and Dolly were staying safely at home with Serenity and her mother. "Jacqueline, how's everything going over there?"

Serenity's mother laughed softly. "The twins are napping. So is Serenity. And we've been having the time of our lives with them, Grant. They're so sweet, so dear, so funny. And Timmy called Serenity Mommy this afternoon."

Mommy. A word that had never been in the twins' vocabulary before. "I hope that made her smile."

"Smile and cry."

Of course. But then Jacqueline went on, "Happy tears, Grant. Your grace and forgiveness have given my daughter the chance I feared she'd never have. To see her children. To be a mother, if only for a short time. Thank you."

His heart went tight. His hands stilled over

the half-tied tie, and then he sighed. "You're welcome, Jacqueline."

"Go," she urged. "Have fun and celebrate your family. Celebrate life. Celebrate love. It's too dear and fleeting to take for granted."

She was right. He said goodbye, finished getting ready and moved down the hall. The chapel entrance was to his left. The bridal room was near Steve Gallagher's office just to the right of the chapel. He walked down the hall with his father, and knocked on the bride's area door.

Emily opened the door, saw him and stood still. Her eyes met his, a gaze of sweet yearning, the same longing that rose within him, as if today of all days it was too hard to hold back. He smiled down at her, then motioned his father into the doorway. "Em, I'd like you to meet someone who's come a long way to do a very special job. He's here to walk the bride down the aisle."

Christa swung around from where Tillie and Janet from the bridal salon were fussing with her veil. "Dad?"

Joe smiled and walked through the door. "Is this okay with you, Christa?"

"Oh, it's more than okay." Quick tears filled her eyes, then slipped in rapid-fire fashion down her cheeks. "It's perfect!"

"Don't cry, you'll muss your makeup!"

"Oh, let her cry, Tillie, it's nothin' we can't fix!"

"Oh, Dad!"

Joe hugged her, and when Emily put her hand on Grant's arm, he laid his own over hers. "You did this."

He shrugged. "It's what I should have done from the beginning."

"God doesn't care that we make mistakes. He cares that we fix them. This is wonderful, Grant." The joyous bridal scene deepened her smile. "Just wonderful."

"I blame you."

"Me?" She wrinkled her forehead and held his gaze.

"You make me want to be a better person, Emily Gallagher."

His words made her smile. She put her second hand on top of his. "Do I?"

"Yes. And I'll have you know it's been a somewhat painful process." He tipped a wry glance down, then indicated the happy reunion. "You inspired this. I hope you're happy."

She looked happy. And proud. Proud of him.

He leaned down and placed a gentle kiss to her forehead, a whisper of a kiss. A promise. "I'm a work in progress, but I think there's hope for me yet."

"There's always hope." Kimberly appeared behind him and tapped her wrist. "Five-minute warning. Are we ready?"

"Yes." Christa smiled up at her dad as Janet fixed her smudged makeup. "We're ready."

"Can I sit in back with you?" Grant asked.

Emily shook her head. "No, you belong up front, but since Kimberly is here to take the rear post, I would be honored to sit up front with you, Grant. If that's all right."

All right?

The month before he'd put pain in her eyes through thoughtless actions. She'd walked away, and Grant had been pretty sure she wouldn't be walking back anytime soon. Her strength showed his weakness and set the bar high. She was right—forgiveness was the key to peace of mind, peace of heart. He laid his hand over hers and moved toward the door. "It's not all right, Em. It's perfect."

He held her hand through the heartfelt service, and when it was over, Grant had made another decision, one that meant everything to him. He didn't want Emily to leave Grace Haven. He didn't want her to dash off to some big city, impressing big-league buyers with her snappy style and savvy decisions.

Was it selfish to want her here, with him? With the kids?

No. It was just plain right. She fit here. She belonged here. And one way or another, he aimed to convince her of that.

He caught her hand later, when the bride and groom finished cutting their cake. She turned, and the smile she gave him made him feel ten feet high. "Are you free in the morning?"

She made a face. "After church, possibly."

"I meant *for* church."

She paused and studied him, as if assessing his sincerity. "I'd like to take Timmy and Dolly," he went on, "but I don't want to do it alone. Would you—"

She didn't wait for him to ask the question. She nodded and clapped her hand over his. "I'd be happy to go to church with you, Grant McCarthy."

"Yeah?" She was looking up at him, purposefully, and the light in her eyes made him feel bigger. Stronger. "It might be a total disaster."

"Possibly, but when they get used to going regularly, they'll be fine. And with both of us there, the odds are with us. Two against two." She smiled at him, and that simple gesture made a good day that much better. "Can we bundle them up and take them to the Winterfest in the park afterward?"

He hadn't been to the town's winter celebration in over a decade. His bad, for keeping himself outside the hustle and bustle of the sweet town he called home. "I'll bring their things."

"Excellent."

He held her gaze. His grip on her hand tightened. More than anything, he longed to dip his head. Touch his lips to hers. Kiss her senseless.

"Oops, there's my cue to organize the dances." She slipped her hand out from under his, but touched his fingers one last, quick time, then stood on tiptoe and whispered, "We'll revisit that idea tomorrow, okay?"

Christa's wedding came first. He smiled and nodded, because she was right. Today was Christa's day, as it should be. But tomorrow, and every day thereafter, he intended to see about winning Emily Gallagher's heart. Starting with a church service and a winter afternoon in the park.

Chapter Sixteen

"Aren't you nervous?" Grant asked when Emily climbed into the front seat of his SUV the next morning.

"Not when you're nervous enough for both of us," she told him. She turned and smiled at the twins. "Good morning, gingersnaps!"

"Mo mo!" Dolly waved two hands in excitement.

"Mornin'." Timmy giggled the word, then wriggled in his seat. "I get out now."

"Soon," she promised. They pulled into the church parking lot a few minutes later and parked next to Corinne's car. Emily climbed out and unbuckled Dolly. Grant did the same with Timmy. And when they met at the front of the SUV, he paused. "If they get disruptive…"

"We'll handle it." She patted his cheek and

started forward. "Let go and let God, Grant. Remember?"

He was learning to do that, but he wasn't sure if his growing faith had a whole lot of influence on toddler behaviors. And then they walked into the old stone church.

"Grant, hello! Good morning. Oh look here, you brought the babies!" Bertie Engle seemed delighted to see them. Hi clapped him on the back with a smile of approval.

"Emily, look how Dolly has grown." Gabby Gallagher grinned when she spotted them. "Sit in front of me. That way if you need help, Rachel and I are here."

"Thank you, Aunt Gabby." Emily slid in, set the diaper bag down and unfastened Dolly's coat. When she slid the toddler's coat off, Rachel sighed out loud.

"Emily, that is like the cutest dress in the world, isn't it?"

"Aunt Tillie got it for her. Super adorable, right?"

"Precious." Gabby whispered the word as she eyed the twins. "So very precious."

They made it through the service with only a couple of minor squabbles, and then they stopped by the Gallagher house to bundle the twins into Winterfest-friendly clothing. Rory had unearthed two plastic sleds from the rafters of the carriage house, and they had to re-strategize toddler seating to fit the sleds into the SUV, but they succeeded eventually. As they pulled into a parking spot off Upper Park Road, Joe McCarthy and his family waved from the sidewalk beyond.

Emily turned toward Grant, surprised. "You invited them to come."

"It's a grandfather's prerogative to take little kids sledding, isn't it? They're here for five days, and I want the kids to enjoy every minute of it."

They slid, they sledded, they drank hot chocolate and gobbled roasted hot dogs and hot, buttered popcorn. When nap time rolled around, Joe offered to take the kids back home. "If I take your car, there's plenty of room for all of us, and we can angle the sleds into the rental."

A few weeks ago, Grant wouldn't have considered handing over the reins to anyone else. This time he agreed happily. Serenity was at the house with her mother, and she'd be happy to tuck the kids in for their naps. "It sounds perfect. That way I get some time alone with my girl."

His girl?

Emily turned and looked up at him as his father waved and pulled away. "Grant, I—"

"Hush." He smiled down at her, put one finger beneath her chin and bent to kiss her. The kiss should have been brief. There were people around, sledding, ice-skating, walking to and from the parking lot.

But she didn't want it to be brief. She wanted it to be at least forever, and possibly more if she could get it. When Grant finally ended the kiss, he pulled her close. So close. And he held her that way, in his embrace, his chin to her hair. "This is how I want things to be, Em."

"Hmm?"

"Just like this," he whispered. "You here, with me. In my arms. Every day, every night. So I'm going to do everything I can to convince you to stay. That's my goal, Emily Gallagher. To convince you to stay in Grace Haven." He leaned down and kissed her again, slow and sweet. "And become my wife. No matter how long it takes. Just so you know."

She leaned back against his arms. "What happens if I'm already committed to staying in Grace Haven?"

His mouth dropped open. His eyebrows shot up. "Do you mean it?"

"Meet Emily Gallagher, the new almost-owner of Caroline's Bridal Salon."

"You're buying the bridal store?" He sounded surprised and delighted.

"I am. That way Kimberly and I can work together as needed, I get to immerse myself in the side of bridal I love, Janet gets to keep a job she loves and I get to live in the sweetest, most wonderful town ever."

He cradled her face in his hands, and Emily was pretty sure she'd never seen a happier man. He kissed her, then hugged her again. "Which means I get to go straight to the proposal."

She laughed, then sighed when Grant went down on one knee, creating quite a stir with the people around them. "Emily Gallagher, will you do me the honor of becoming my wife and being a mother to my two adorable if somewhat naughty children?"

People paused.

Some whispered.

Excited looks went back and forth, and when Emily put her hand on his cheek and nodded yes, the small crowd cheered.

Grant stood, grabbed her up in a hug and whirled her around, then he fist-pumped the air. And when he finally set her down, he sealed the deal with one more long, sweet kiss.

"But Grant." She faced him seriously as they strolled through the forest paths for one last afternoon walk before going home. "Despite the fact that we want to move fast, I think we need to take this slow. Kind of."

"Because of Serenity's situation."

"Yes." She nodded, relieved. "Her time is short. God willing, ours isn't. So can we keep this on the down low for a little bit?"

He put one arm around her shoulders and tugged her in. "Yes. It's a small enough sacrifice."

It was, and his words made her smile.

A few months ago, Grant wouldn't have said those words, or thought twice about the timing. Now he not only considered others, he cared about the consequences, and that only made her love him more. "But let's agree on one thing, okay?"

"What's that, darlin'?"

She faced him, grabbed his leather bomber jacket and pulled him close. "I want a small wedding, and by small I mean so small our budgets don't even know it happened. Family, kids, Uncle Steve, done. Agreed?"

He laughed out loud. "Since we're going to be surrounded by weddings for the forseeable future, I'm absolutely fine with that. I love you, Em."

A light snow started falling just then. Nothing major, just tiny flakes, floating straight down, without a breath of wind. She looked up at Grant, with the snow sifting around him, and said, "I love you, too."

They stood just like that for long seconds, smiling at each other, the snow falling gently, and then Grant took her hand and led her toward the SUV. "Let's go home, darlin'."

Epilogue

Grant looked up, surprised and really happy to see his bride-to-be three short hours before their wedding. He crossed the lawn, reached out his arms and drew her in once she climbed out of her SUV. "I thought the groom wasn't allowed to see the bride before the wedding?"

"I've got my own set of rules," she assured him, and he laughed, because he knew the truth in that. "I had to show you something. I couldn't wait. It just arrived in the mail."

He waited as she slipped a glossy book from a small box. She handed it to him and watched as he stared at the cover. *"Mommy and Me."* He whispered the words, gazing at the cover pic of the twins' mother, holding them the past winter, all three faces filled with joy. "They look so happy."

"Yes." She nodded eagerly as he went through

the book, page by page. "This is my wedding present to the kids. This is Timmy's version. I created a book for each of them through an online site, so they'll both have books of them with Serenity."

"This is amazing, Em." But then, she was amazing, so why was he surprised? "They'll treasure these forever."

"Well, the good thing is that if they ruin them somehow, I ordered double. One to cherish and see, and one to have tucked away." She reached out and put her hand on his arm. "I wanted today to be a new and wonderful beginning for all four of us. But I also want the kids to grow up knowing how much their mother loved them before she died."

"She did, didn't she?" Grant stared at the book. He had to blink hard, twice, but then he put his arms around Emily and drew her into his heart, his chest. "You make a difference, Em, everywhere you go, and I'm going to spend the rest of my life thanking God for putting you in my path last fall."

"When you're not being stubborn," she added cheerfully.

He laughed, because that was true. "I love you, Em." He kissed her, long and slow, and then sighed. "And I'm glad you don't mind an at-home honeymoon."

"Best kind of all," she told him. "Because I'll be with you and the kids." She pressed the books into his hands. "Tuck those away for now and I will see you—" she glanced at her phone and winced. "In two hours and fifteen minutes, which means I really should go home and get ready."

"You can show up looking just like that." He swept her jeans and T-shirt a quick smile. "As long as you say *I do* at the proper time, it's all good." He followed her to the SUV, leaned in and kissed her one last time. "See you soon. And then you're stuck with me, Em."

"I know." She laughed softly, reached out and hugged him. "Isn't it the most marvelous feeling ever?"

It was, he realized as she pulled away. He'd been so sure he was right, in so many ways...

And then God put Emily in front of him, filled with thoughts and ideas and kindness. She blessed him in ways he'd have never thought possible. But God did.

"No, Dowwy! Nooo!" Timmy's shriek sent Grant running.

"Wheeeeee!" Dolly's peal of delight made him laugh as he raced to the backyard for whatever was going on.

"Grant, we might have a little problem here,"

Percy called. He ambled forward, followed by two soaking-wet kids. "But on the plus side, Dolly's learned how to turn on the hose."

He bent and scooped up Dolly, congratulating her, and then took both kids inside to get cleaned up.

He'd faced raising them alone, and now God had given him a helpmate, a kind, funny, strong wife and mother to his children, and judging from their antics today?

God sent her at the perfect time.

He showed up at the church with the kids at the appointed time, but only because Aunt Tillie was right there, helping.

"I've got dibs on Dolly!" Rory scooped Dolly up and twirled her around. "Hi, sweet cheeks!"

Dolly giggled and patted Rory's face. "Wo! Wuv ooo!"

"Oh, how amazingly darling is that?" Rory laughed and hugged the little girl. "And I love your pretty dress, Doll-face."

"Grant, we need you up front." Kimberly hailed him from the broad steps of the abbey.

"Of course." He took his place at the sanctuary. Rory settled Dolly in the pew with her parents. Joe and Linda were reading a story to Timmy. The small gathering of family and friends all sat toward the front of the abbey's chapel. The flutist began playing fun, dancing notes, welcoming the bride.

The guests stood.

Timmy spotted Emily right off. "Em!" he yelled, waving to get her attention. Oh, he got it, all right. "I got wet! Dowwy spwayed me!" He scrambled off Joe's lap and dashed down the aisle to tell Emily all about their morning adventure.

She bent low, flashed Grant a smile—a smile that said she was absolutely ready to sign on for life—and took Tim's hand to make him part of the procession with her father.

"Me, too!" Dolly hung out into the aisle, arms out, begging, once she spotted her brother.

Emily didn't hesitate. She handed Rory the small bouquet of flowers, settled Dolly on her hip and walked the last few steps with a toddler in her arms and one by her side. "We're here."

Grant laughed, picked Timmy up and faced her uncle Steve, the abbey's pastor. "It looks like we're ready."

The congregation laughed, Steve Gallagher grinned and when Emily slanted a smile up to Grant, his heart went soft with love.

He'd stopped counting his blessings when he was a little kid. He'd started again, once Emily charged into his life. And now—

He kissed Tim's sweet cheek as he nodded and said "I do" at the appropriate time.

Now he had it all, and he'd never take that for granted again.

* * * * *

*If you loved this story,
pick up the first* GRACE HAVEN *book,
AN UNEXPECTED GROOM.*

*And check out these other stories
of small-town life
from author Ruth Logan Herne's previous
miniseries,* KIRKWOOD LAKE:

*THE LAWMAN'S HOLIDAY WISH
LOVING THE LAWMAN
HER HOLIDAY FAMILY
HEALING THE LAWMAN'S HEART*

Available now from Love Inspired!

*Find more great reads at
www.LoveInspired.com.*

Dear Reader,

I can't tell you how much I loved writing this book. First, I'm blessed by the beautiful Finger Lakes setting for Grace Haven. I don't know of a prettier area anywhere, a land dotted with forest, farm and fun, with sources of water offering food and frolic and God's simple beauty. Did you know that they're called the Finger Lakes because it looks like God nestled his righteous hand right into the beauty of the earth? Of course it was probably glaciers, but I'll always err on the side of the more romantic notion! And those twins, Dolly and Timmy??? Be still my heart!

I have to thank my editor, Melissa Endlich, for her wisdom on this book. She helped me see Emily Gallagher more clearly, and her input made this story sparkle. It's not easy being the middle sister. It's tough to live up to such high standards, and no one pats you on the head like they do to the adorable baby sister. And Emily's pageant success made some people see her as one-dimensional. Nothing could be further from the truth, but Emily has to prove it, and that's not always easy in a small town. Emily comes into this story determined to show others what she's known all along. That she's strong in her own right.

Grant McCarthy's confusion comes from multiple sources. A Christian mother who didn't live as she preached, a longtime grudge that grew stronger with time and trusting the wrong people. As he unwinds the tangled threads of his mistrust, he sees that God was there all the time, always lingering in the truth, just where you'd expect Him to be. And Grant comes to win Emily's love when he takes a breath, shoves pride and anger aside, and forgives others the way he knows he should.

I hope you love their story, a hard-working highwayman and a beauty queen, and their willingness to become stronger, better people, and more perfect for one another.

I love hearing from readers! You can email me at loganherne@gmail.com, and please come friend me on Facebook, where I love to chat and pray and play! Visit my website at www.ruthloganherne.com and as always, thank you so much for taking the time to read this book. I am most grateful!

Ruthy